W
Temmi   n

Because Temmi was not looking for an adventure, it did not mean that an adventure was not looking for him. ~~that very~~ *that very moment in the shape of a terrifyingly large bull-troll and a plain, usual-sized wizard.*

When Agna fled from the High Witchlands, she brought the magic Icicle with her, a present from the Witch-Queen. But Icicle is the Frost Dragon's lodestone, and there is a curse on it which threatens the safety of the village. The only way to get rid of the curse is to return Icicle to the dragon, before the next full moon.

With the wizard's help, Temmi, Agna, and Cush start their long and frightening journey to the dragon's mountain. On the way they meet scary new enemies—and even scarier old ones . . .

Stephen Elboz lives in Northamptonshire, and has had a variety of jobs, including being a dustman, a civil servant, and a volunteer on an archaeological dig. He now divides his time between teaching and writing. His first book, *The House of Rats*, won the Smarties Young Judges Prize and his series of books about the young magician Kit Stixby have earned him great critical acclaim.

Temmi and the Frost Dragon

Other books by Stephen Elboz

Temmi and the
Frost Dragon

Stephen Elboz

Illustrated by Lesley Harker

OXFORD
UNIVERSITY PRESS

For Max Davies Winkworth
because he likes dwarfs

Special thanks to
Linda 'dancing fingers' Hitchens

OXFORD
UNIVERSITY PRESS

Great Clarendon Street, Oxford OX2 6DP

Oxford University Press is a department of the University of Oxford.
It furthers the University's objective of excellence in research, scholarship,
and education by publishing worldwide in

Oxford New York

Auckland Bangkok Buenos Aires
Cape Town Chennai Dar es Salaam Delhi Hong Kong Istanbul
Karachi Kolkata Kuala Lumpur Madrid Melbourne Mexico City Mumbai
Nairobi São Paulo Shanghai Taipei Tokyo Toronto

Oxford is a registered trade mark of Oxford University Press
in the UK and in certain other countries

British Library Cataloguing in Publication Data available

ISBN 0 19 275252 9

1 3 5 7 9 10 8 6 4 2

Typeset by AFS Image Setters Ltd, Glasgow

Printed in Great Britain by
Cox & Wyman Ltd, Reading, Berkshire

Chapter One

After his last adventure, Temmi honestly thought he would never go on another one—or at least not another one quite as grand as that adventure had been. After all, he told himself, one big adventure in a lifetime is more than most people ever have, so he didn't really mind too much. Indeed, he was happy enough living an ordinary life in an ordinary village, doing ordinary everyday things that needed to be done, such as fishing the lake and mending the nets.

He lived in a small thatched hut with his father; and his friends lived nearby in plain thatched huts similar to his own—although it must be said his friends were far from ordinary. Wormlugs,

Crumbtoot, Mudsniff, Flywick, and Kobble were five rather quarrelsome dwarfs; while Agna had spent most of her life as a princess in a witch's castle . . . And then, of course, there was Cush, a flying bear, who Temmi loved as much as any living creature.

So, all in all, Temmi had a lot to be grateful for, and there was much to be said for just staying at home and being a simple fisherman's son, especially when the rain was beating on the thatch, or it blew cold, or he had just awoken from a nightmare about his old enemy General Tin Nose, seeing him in a dream, his false nose glinting and Frostbite his wolf by his side.

And if there was not to be another adventure, Temmi's story might well turn out so dull (to us, at any rate) that there would be no point in telling it . . .

. . . Ah, but it was not to be that way. Because Temmi was not looking for an adventure, it did not mean that an adventure was not looking for *him*. Indeed, one was charging straight towards him right at that very moment, in the shape of a terrifyingly large bull-troll and a plain, usual-sized wizard.

The-morning-that-was-supposed-to-be-like-all-the-others-but-wouldn't-be started well enough. It was high summer, and the fishing could be done early because the days were so long. Temmi was glad about this because it meant the rest of the day was his to visit Cush, who lived away in the forest just where the mountains began, in a colony of flying bears all as white as he was.

Temmi climbed up through the trees; he had come this way so often that his feet had worn their own track.

'Come on,' he called impatiently, turning to wait for Agna.

She stopped to wipe her brow on the back of her hand. 'It's hot—what's the rush?' But she knew Temmi was always eager to see Cush. Usually the dwarfs came along too and it was more often they who did the grumbling about being hurried. But not today. Temmi had asked them to come, of course, but when he had they had gone unexpectedly quiet.

'Haven't you heard?' whispered Kobble. 'There's something big roaming the forest. It might be a growler.'

'So?' shrugged Temmi. 'Growlers may be the meanest bears who ever lived, but they won't harm you if you stay out of their way.'

'Yes they will,' snapped Wormlugs, chewing on his pipe. 'I happen to know for a fact that growlers are particularly fond of dwarf meat, and it's bound to be me who gets eaten first—I'm the biggest and oldest.'

'Biggest and chewiest, you mean,' cried Mudsniff, setting off all the other dwarfs shouting how much better a meal they would make for a hungry growler.

They were still arguing about it when Agna and Temmi slipped away, sighing and raising their eyes in despair. And now they were deep into the forest and the lake was a distant gleam between the trees as they climbed ever higher.

Just then Agna stopped and looked around.

'What's the matter?' asked Temmi, still waiting for her to catch up. 'That's the third time you've stopped like that. Have you heard Kobble's growler?'

He was amused because of the two of them *he* was the hunter: he would have heard a prowling creature long before Agna. But he had forgotten that Agna had special gifts of her own, she knew about the ways of magic.

'Oh . . . it's nothing,' she said hurrying up to him, but still looking around. 'Perhaps it's the

4

weather. When it gets very hot it can feel as if the sky is pressing down on you.'

'Is that how you feel now?' asked Temmi.

Agna smiled. 'Come on,' she said. 'Let's see who spots a flying bear first.'

Together they tramped on, Temmi watching Agna from the corner of his eye, and Agna watching the forest as if unsure of it, as if it might spring a surprise on her. And in the end it did exactly that.

'Temmi, *look*,' she gasped.

Temmi saw something among the branches but didn't really understand what, until they came up close to it. Then he was rather alarmed. On a stick pushed into the ground he saw a deer's skull— grinning and sun-bleached. And if this was not sinister enough in his view, hung here and there from its antlers were little tufts of dried moss and feathers, and neatly bound parcels made of leaves, and metal bells that tinkled as they approached. Around the skull's eye-holes he saw strange painted symbols; others were scratched on to its teeth.

'When did *that* appear?' he whispered. 'It wasn't here last time we came.'

Agna wasn't listening. She reached out her hand to the skull and the bells tinkled madly until she took her hand away.

5

'This is strong magic, Temmi,' she said.

Temmi blinked nervously at the skull; it wasn't something he understood or liked. 'Bad magic, do you think?'

'No . . . at least it doesn't *feel* bad. It's a kind of protecting magic. It makes an invisible wall. See, it runs from the skull to that bunch of mistletoe over there, and I expect on through other magic tokens we can't see from here. It might even go all the way round our village.'

'Who could have put it here?' wondered Temmi.

'Nobody we know, that's for sure.'

Temmi frowned: at that moment he was in two minds whether to turn straight back to the village and report their find, or go on. Yet despite the scary look of the skull, Agna assured him it wasn't anything evil or dangerous, besides which he was anxious to see that no harm had come to the flying bears, so he decided they should go on. And a short while later they stepped out of the forest into a daisy-flecked meadow and spotted a flying bear. It was Cush. And he was looking out for them as much as they were looking out for him.

'Cush! Cush!' shouted Temmi waving his arm in the air, but he had long since been spotted, Cush diving down like a white spark spat from the sun. He landed between the two youngsters, his stubby tail a blur and his nose snuffling about Temmi's bag for the fish inside.

'You little thief, try to rob me, would you?' laughed Temmi. Playfully he wrestled Cush to the ground, Cush nipping him gently as they rolled over and over.

Then they fell apart and sat gazing adoringly at each other.

Cush was now just over a year old and although Temmi had seen the span of his wings more than double in that time, he was still the smallest of the cubs born the previous year; and whenever Temmi hugged him, he could feel the bones beneath his thick, white fur.

'All right,' said Temmi clambering on to Cush's back, 'if you want your fish so badly, you can earn it. Give me a ride.'

Pulling the fish from his bag he dangled it teasingly before Cush's nose, but whipped it away before Cush could claw it out of his hand. Cush yowled and made a pretence of being angry—but that was all part of their game. Stretching wide his snowy wings, he beat them hard until Temmi felt himself lifting into the wide blue sky, seeing Agna grow small as she squinted up at him, and the forest rolling away to misty mountains in the distance.

They rose higher and for no good reason at all Temmi laughed as a cool breeze blew against his face. He felt special—he felt he was king of the world. But he had no wish to wear out the little half-grown bear.

'Very well,' he said. 'You've earned your fish. You can take me down now.'

To his surprise, Cush's wings kept up their steady beat, and Temmi realized that the bear hadn't paid him the slightest attention.

'Land, Cush,' he said more firmly.

Cush, however, continued to hover. Beneath his hands, Temmi felt Cush's fur slowly rise, turning prickly against his skin. Cush was staring down, his eyes fixed to something far below in the forest. It was not something he liked. He began to growl and Temmi felt the sound travel the whole length of the flying bear's body.

'Cush?'

Shifting slightly, Temmi managed to peer over Cush's side; it was difficult to see. As Cush's wings rose and fell, his eyes moved quickly, at last catching a distant movement—a stirring in the trees. Then a few wing beats later he too saw what Cush had seen and his stomach gave a violent lurch.

Like a thing of ragged shadows clumsily

stitched together, a huge dark blot was making its way through the trees towards Agna, who stood innocently staring up at him as he rode Cush, shading her eyes against the brilliant white sun. Wriggling hard, Temmi got himself into a better position to view the dark shape again. His heart beat faster as he picked it out. Although he had never come across one before, he knew from tales told at the longhouse that the blob was a troll come up from the Underworld. And, as he watched, the troll effortlessly uprooted a fully grown tree, and lurched on ever closer to Agna.

'Agna!' yelled Temmi, the shout exploding from his mouth. 'Agna—run! Get away!'

He saw her smile and wave up at him. He was too high for her to catch anything of his warning: she thought he was calling to be noticed.

The troll was stalking her, Temmi could see that now, steadily bulldozing its way towards the edge of the trees; and a bitter thought came to him. The dwarfs' mysterious creature hadn't been a growler at all. It had been something far worse. And at a time that called for spears, and bows and arrows, all Temmi had in his hand was a stupid fish. Nevertheless he took aim and hurled it as hard as he could. The shot couldn't have been better. It struck the troll on the head and, a few seconds later when its tiny brain realized, it raised its face to the sky.

'Oh!'

Temmi jerked back in surprise, the troll's glare as unexpected as a slap—a blaze of sudden fury. Now it stared up at him, Temmi saw the troll's hog-like tusks and marvelled at their size and the way they pulled the creature's mouth into a shapeless gash which could not close, and from which globs of drool endlessly dripped. Between the tusks was a whole shark's bite of jagged teeth. Beyond that, as far as Temmi could judge, the troll was all tightly knotted muscle and coarse bristly hair.

Turning away from Temmi, the troll furiously stamped the fish underfoot (as if showing what it would do to Temmi if ever it caught him) then it was off again, closing the distance on Agna— who *still* did not realize the danger.

Temmi boiled with determination to help her.

'Land, Cush. Take me down now!' His voice sounded thick at the back of his throat.

But every part of Cush told him that this was exactly what *not* to do. Instinct told him that he was safe from the troll so long as he stayed in the air. Temmi could shout and plead as much as he liked, but nothing would make him change his mind.

Temmi sat still, thinking quickly. He couldn't very well be angry with Cush for being a bear and acting like one. But he had to reach Agna somehow, even if it meant doing something reckless like forcing Cush down.

This decided, he began to struggle and bounce his weight up and down on Cush's back, until Cush had no choice but to spread his wings to steady himself. As Temmi hoped, the moment he did he began to glide to earth, picking up speed alarmingly. He came down hard and all of a sudden. Not quite prepared for the jolt, Temmi was thrown off his back. The hardness of the ground shocked him. And rolling over and over through the long meadow grass, he finally came to a stop at Agna's feet, bruised, dazed, and breathless.

She laughed at his clowning (as she thought it)—but not for long. Hearing crackling wood she turned to the trees. It was then—before Temmi could say a word—that the forest burst open showering the ground with shredded leaves and strips of bark—and there was the troll, panting hard; staring at them with its tiny flinty eyes.

Agna gave a scream of horror, her eyes stretched wide.

The troll roared ten times louder, drool flying from its lips like spray in a storm.

Then it launched itself at them, moving at incredible speed for something so large and awkward.

Jumping up, Temmi grabbed Agna. After that he couldn't move—he just froze with terror. His throat tightened. He couldn't make a sound. He even forgot to breathe. He could only watch helplessly as the creature came thundering straight towards them. *Tusks, hair, muscle—*

And that should have been an end to it. Or rather an end to them. They should have been troll meat—chewed and swallowed. Except just then there came a blinding flash and a deafening blast, which shook the air almost as much as the ground was shaken as the great troll dropped down dead—its twisted tusks ploughing up the earth into a mound.

The flash left the scene lost in thick rolling smoke. Through it and the strange silence it brought with it, arose a voice.

'Um . . . If I may take the chance of introducing myself. My name is Ollimun Nubb. I am a wizard. Look, sorry about the smoke.'

Chapter Two

The smoke cleared slowly and, as it did, Temmi was struck by two surprising things. The first was that he and Agna had somehow managed to curl up in a ball on the ground together for their own safety. The second was that the lifeless troll lay only a matter of a few steps away. In fact the troll was so close that as Temmi got to his feet he could plainly see its pale skin beneath the masses of thick, coarse hair, along with many ugly battle scars and scabs where the hair had worn thin.

The troll's body made an untidy heap on the ground, and the stranger who called himself Ollimun Nubb was to be seen climbing up on to its shoulder, pulling himself up with his tall wand, which still smoked a little after blasting the troll with magic.

'Quite a fine view up here,' he said mildly, looking at it for a while before picking his way back down. He tugged out one of the troll's mighty arms and sat on it, his back against the troll's flank, at perfect peace with the still-warm monster.

'As you can see,' he said struggling to lift the troll's wrist to show them its paw, 'fresh mud beneath its claws. I'd say this one had only just dug its way out of the Underworld. It is not the first to do so, nor will it be the last.'

Letting the paw flop back down with a thud, he dusted his hands together.

'We must speak,' he said glancing up at Temmi and Agna. 'Pull up a paw and sit down.'

'Please, sir,' said Temmi, much in awe of him. 'If you don't mind, sir, I'd rather sit on the ground.'

'Sit where you please, it is the talk that matters most.'

Temmi and Agna crept forward; Agna still trembling and Temmi not quite over his shock either—but curious to hear what the wizard had to say. They sat in the long grass before Ollimun Nubb who was like a king on a troll throne. As for Cush, he took much longer to settle. Restlessly he sniffed all around the troll to make sure no spark of life was left in it, and when certain there wasn't, he came and lay down beside Temmi.

'We . . . we don't often see wizards around here,' said Temmi, as if giving himself an excuse to stare at the stranger—who was certainly *stranger* than anyone Temmi and Agna had ever seen before.

He, the stranger, this Ollimun Nubb, was a big shaggy man, his cloak made out of patches of different furs and skins, the faded embroidery on his gown coming undone. Around his middle was a broad belt, and hanging from this on strings, ribbons, or strips of leather, they noticed a variety of eye-catching objects. Bones, and stones with perfectly round holes in them, and tiny bottles woven around in wicker, and bunches of dried herbs, and knobbly roots and little silk printed bags, as well as plain pouches for more everyday items like needles and handkerchiefs and crusts of bread.

Yet even more wizardly than what he wore were the marks upon his face—a crescent moon tattooed around his left eye, a sun around his right; while nestling in the dimple of his chin was a small blue star. Colourful beads were threaded

on to his beard and his hair was long, some strands tightly plaited. Like a tree, it was impossible to guess his age, although his teeth were long and yellow like an old mule's. And, close to, he smelt . . . well, thought Agna, he smelt a bit like an old mule too.

Ollimun Nubb knew he was being studied from head to toe. He was used to it and considered it perfectly normal for ordinary folk to stare. And for that purpose he laid his wand across his knees so Temmi and Agna might have a better view of the designs upon it, seeing there a sun and moon at either end, similar to the tattoos upon his face—the moon in copper, the sun in ancient gold. The wizard sat very still waiting patiently until both curious youngsters were done.

'There,' he said, waving away the flies that had already begun to gather, buzzing in a cloud around the troll's ears. 'Now you know more about me than I do about you. Time you told me something about yourselves. Start with your names, that will be enough to begin with . . . *Boy*—you first.'

'Temmi, sir,' answered Temmi at once. 'Short for Temmithia.'

'And I'm Agna,' said she when he pointed his wand at her.

He nodded, satisfied. 'And the creature?'

'This is Cush,' said Temmi, hugging him. 'He's a flying bear.'

'So I see. It's quite a day for strange creatures. Luckily for flying bears and unluckily for trolls, I happen to know the good ones from the bad.'

Abruptly Agna said, 'It was you who put the protection around our village, wasn't it?'

'It was.'

'Why?'

For his answer Ollimun Nubb patted the troll. 'It will keep out the likes of him and his friends—at least for a while.'

Temmi frowned up at the troll's great muscles, considering the frightening strength that once it had.

'We nearly ended up as its dinner,' he said.

'Perhaps,' said the wizard coolly turning his gaze on Agna. 'It certainly meant to harm *you*, child. And possibly for the very same thing I can sense on you too.'

Temmi and Agna looked at each other, puzzled. The wizard went on.

'You have about you some object of great magical power.'

'No—' Agna started to say when she remembered a small trinket given to her by the

Witch-Queen of the High Witchlands when Agna was a princess there.

'Oh, you mean this,' she said taking out a small object of clearest ice. 'I call it Icicle—the ice never melts.'

'And it does do magic,' said Temmi. 'At the Witch's castle it helped us to escape, didn't it, Agna?'

She nodded. 'That was the last time I used it.'

Looking at him, it was hard for Temmi to judge what Ollimun Nubb was thinking just then, but certainly it was deep thoughts. He stretched out a hand, snake-skin bracelets on his wrist.

'May I?'

Agna glanced at Temmi who shrugged a *why not?*, then handed it over.

Carefully the wizard held up Icicle to the sun, examining every part of it. And then for closer inspection he put on a peculiar pair of spectacles which had a movable magnifying glass set into the frames: this he slid from his moon eye to his sun eye and back again, so one eye was always made to appear much larger than the other.

'Did the Witch tell you anything about it?' he asked looking at Agna, his moon eye three times the size of his sun eye.

Agna shook her head. 'Only that it was precious

and would do magic for me, and one day I would find out just how great its powers are.'

'Did she ever warn you *not* to take it away from her lands?'

'No, but when she gave it to me she never expected I would leave her castle. Why do you ask? What is it that's so special about Icicle?'

Temmi heard Ollimun Nubb splutter. '*Icicle*. Such a childish name. *It is not an icicle*. Nor is it something to be tucked away in your pocket like a toy. It is a dragon's lodestone, and it may surprise you to know that if you blow it like a horn it will summon a dragon.'

He saw the two youngsters look puzzled. He sighed.

'You do know about dragons, don't you?'

'Of course,' replied Temmi happily. 'They are big creatures and quite fierce too, so I'm told.'

For a second time he heard Ollimun Nubb splutter. *Big-and-quite-fierce* . . . Ho, boy, they are *gigantic*! They are *fer-ocious*! They are the lord-king-emperor of every other living thing!' He sounded so excited that Cush lifted his head to stare at him. 'Neither good nor bad, they live for centuries and are almost impossible to kill. However, they have two weaknesses. The first is their love of treasure. Each dragon has its own treasure store, and every full moon must fly off to find more. The second weakness is much more complex . . . When a dragon hatches from its egg there is always one object more precious to it than a whole mountainful of ordinary treasure—*its lodestone*. I have known it to be a ring, or a lantern, or a sword. It may be something worth only a few pennies to you or me, but to a dragon it is priceless. You see, whoever owns that lodestone becomes the dragon's master.'

'And Icicle is one of these special objects?' whispered Agna, hugging her knees in excitement.

'Indeed. It belongs to a frost dragon called Grimskalk and was stolen from her many years ago by the old Witch-Queen. Grimskalk has been desperate to get it back ever since.'

'So I have a dragon—a dragon of my very own!'

Ollimun Nubb frowned. 'You would be foolish if you thought you could *own* a dragon—just as you would be unwise to try to use the lodestone to summon Grimskalk to appear. Only those with strong magical powers can ever hope to be master of a dragon. Those who have none are merely left with the dragon's curse.'

This, as well as the wizard's tone of voice, did not sound at all promising.

'What do you mean—*curse?*' asked Agna slowly.

'It is simple. To stop thieves, all dragons' treasure is cursed—the more precious the object the more terrible the curse. When you lived at the Witch's castle, the Witch had her own strong magic to disguise the lodestone and hide it from Grimskalk; more importantly, the Witch's magic prevented the curse from taking hold. Safe in her castle, the lodestone might not have been able to call the dragon, but it was still a marvellous magical object, which is why the Witch gave it to you. Ah, but once you took it away from the protection of her magic, matters changed . . . ' Ollimun Nubb closed his eyes for a moment and to Temmi's surprise he noticed that even his eyelids were tattooed! 'The dragon's curse is like a disease, child, and now it has spread from you to your village. The creatures of the Underworld are beginning to rise—are beginning to creep to the surface. The troll is proof of that. The dragon's curse is giving them the heart to come crawling up from their caves and holes in the deep dark depths below.'

'*Oh.*' Agna's expression dropped. 'In that case I shall get rid of Icicle—I'll get rid of it for good. Temmi will help me, won't you? We'll throw it into the deepest part of the lake—'

'It won't help you one little bit—the curse is too advanced. The only sure way to lift it now is for you—and only you—to return the lodestone to Grimskalk at the next full moon. That's when she is away from her mountain searching for new treasure. There is no other way.'

'None?' said Temmi.

'None,' said Ollimun Nubb firmly. 'Naturally I offer you my services as a guide . . . The question is, are you willing to travel along that long hard road with me?'

Agna didn't know quite what to say.

'What do *you* think?' she asked turning to Temmi.

He rubbed his chin. 'As I see it the choice is between trolls or dragons—or at least *a* dragon.'

This was no help at all to Agna, so for a long time she sat still, thinking hard: and by her expression Temmi knew she was arguing with herself over what she should do. Nobody rushed her.

At last she took back Icicle and put it safely into her pocket.

'Well?' demanded Temmi. 'If you're going to Grimskalk's mountain, I'm coming with you.'

'Good,' she said. 'I was hoping that you would.'

Chapter Three

And so it was decided.

Temmi could not believe so much had happened so quickly.

Beside him Cush whined.

'You'd best say goodbye to him, boy,' said Ollimun Nubb, using his wand to pull himself up from the troll.

'Yes,' said Temmi reluctantly. He hugged the deep fur around Cush's neck, feeling the bear's warm breath in his ear.

'I shall miss you, Cush, I shall miss you every day . . . Just you be sure you stay out of trouble, y'hear? And warn the other bears to be on their guard against trolls and whatever else follows them. Goodbye, boy . . . Goodbye, Cush . . . '

He tightened his hug for a moment and when he moved back, Cush gave him such a knowing look that Temmi wondered if he had understood him.

Then Agna was there, tugging at his shoulder, red faced and sounding angry.

'Temmi, that wizard says we have to set off straight away. He says we can't go home first. But I want to. If we don't, think how everyone will go mad worrying about us.'

'If you return to your village,' said Ollimun Nubb quietly, 'the curse will never be lifted. You will not be allowed to take a single step on the journey to Grimskalk's mountain. Your people will be afraid for you, they will keep you at home believing they are protecting you from danger, which is untrue.'

'But we can't just vanish,' protested Temmi.

Ollimun Nubb nodded understandingly. 'We shall send word at the next village. I promise. And we shall get everything we need for our journey there, too.'

This made sense to Temmi, although like Agna he was far from happy about it. It didn't seem right just to sneak away. He thought of his father waiting for him to return home, growing more and more anxious.

'Poor Pa, he's going to think he's lost me for a second time . . . '

Unwilling and unprepared they set off into the forest, Temmi glancing back for one last glimpse of Cush. For a while they went in silence, neither he nor Agna feeling much like talking. Then the wizard started showing them things they would never have noticed by themselves, and spoke cheerfully to lift their spirits. And eventually it worked. Once they were distracted from their gloomy thoughts, they began to feel growing pangs of real excitement, especially when the wizard spoke of the frost dragon, Grimskalk.

'She is not the largest dragon I have seen, but by no means the smallest either,' he told them. 'For much of the time she sleeps coiled around her mountain top like a serpent. This way she is able to guard the treasure hidden away inside.'

'What, she can guard her treasure while asleep?' said Agna surprised.

'Oh, indeed—asleep. Don't be fooled by a dragon's closed eyes. It is as misleading a thing as a crocodile's smile.'

'A what?' said Temmi.

'A croc—oh, never mind.'

'Going back to Grimskalk a moment,' said Agna ducking to avoid a low branch. 'You say our only chance of reaching the mountain safely is during a full moon when she flies off to search for new treasure?'

Ollimun Nubb nodded. 'Now you see why we cannot waste time. If we miss the next full moon we'll be forced to wait a whole month until the moon grows fat again. And all the while Grimskalk's curse becomes stronger. The Underworldlings are swarming up towards the Overworld. And once here it'll take nothing less than a war to push them back down their holes again.'

Temmi and Agna glanced at each other uneasily.

'And how far away *is* Grimskalk's mountain?' asked Temmi.

'Ten—maybe eleven—days' hard march—and that's if we meet no trouble along the way.'

'That far!' cried Agna. 'But the next full moon is in twelve days' time.'

'Just so,' agreed the wizard calmly. 'Now, can I smell wood smoke?'

They arrived at a village in the forest, and although it lay only five miles away from Temmi's own village, he had never visited it before and the people there were strangers to him.

Everyone turned out to meet them, including the dogs and goats and a whole squawking tribe of dirty, naked infants.

Ollimun Nubb started to do business straight away. He sold charms, cured toothache, read fortunes, gave directions to find a lost billy goat, removed warts, and told expectant mothers if their next baby would be a boy or a girl.

In return he asked for supplies and clothes to fit Agna and Temmi—good warm winter clothes, he said. The villagers happily gave him their children's old winter clothes because there was plenty of time to make new ones before the cold weather set in.

This was not all. Speaking to the whole village, the wizard said, as important as the clothes and supplies, was the favour he was about to ask.

He requested that a band of well-armed men (protected also with charms that he would give them) go to the lake village, with some important news. The news was not good. It concerned a dragon's curse and trolls in the forest and youngsters who had to go on a long dangerous journey to put things right. The wizard was brief and to the point and told the villagers only what they needed to know, managing not to mention Icicle at all. The fewer people who knew about that the better.

The villagers listened in silence. They did not ask a single question. They looked at the ground, they looked at each other—they stopped looking at the wizard.

Temmi, who did not notice this change in them, was busy thinking of his father. He desperately wanted to send a message of his own, and as he could no more write than his pa could read, he quickly scratched a picture of a flying bear on to a piece of bark. It was something he did all the time, so his father would realize it came from him and know he was safe and well. Then he ran to give it to one of the departing men and was struck by how unfriendly he was when he took it: how cold his scowl before he slipped the scrap of wood grudgingly into his pocket.

When the band of men had gone, Temmi quickly found Agna, and soon they became aware of whispers and mutters on all sides.

'There were no trolls around here until that wizard showed up.'

'Perhaps his magic is black magic.'

'Perhaps he stole those poor children and will steal ours given the chance.'

From the corner of his eye, Temmi saw some slip off the charms they had been only too glad to wear a few minutes before.

As it grew dark, the company was given a hut for the night. Not in the village itself, although some huts there were clearly unlived in, but one set back in the forest. Agna wrinkled up her nose. It smelt of cows which was hardly surprising—it was a cow shed, without food, water, or a stick of firewood.

Ollimun Nubb gazed slowly around with a sad smile and showed no surprise.

Full night came and the moon rose. The company went to bed on dirty straw, ignoring the rats fighting and squeaking in the thatch above. Temmi had barely drifted off to sleep when a stone struck the roof and the shouts started.

'Devils!'

'Dirty black magickers!'

'Curse bringers!'

More stones followed the first, hammering on the roof like storm rain.

Agna gave a startled cry. Temmi sat up in alarm. In the darkness they saw Ollimun Nubb standing by the doorway with their bundles, ready to leave.

'We have outstayed our welcome,' he said. 'Gather up your blankets and come here.'

When Agna and Temmi had done what he told them, he said, 'Walk quickly behind me—

but do not run. They shall not chase us away like dogs.'

'But the stones—' began Agna.

'They hurt far less than cruel words. Remember you are under my protection, child. Stay close to my wand.'

Unquestioningly Agna and Temmi followed him outside. In amongst the trees the villagers remained hidden (yet were close judging by the loudness of their voices). The sight of the wizard and his two young companions made them even more furious. Stones were thrown by the dozen. Yet each one stopped short in mid air and fell harmlessly to the ground.

For a time the villagers followed them deeper into the forest, hurling insults and stones at every step, until finally losing interest they returned to their homes. Without their screams and yells the forest was eerily silent.

Ollimun Nubb sighed. 'The night is warm. It will not harm us to sleep beneath the stars.'

'They were so angry,' said Agna turning back to see if anyone still followed them.

'You expected trouble all along, didn't you?' asked Temmi.

Ollimun Nubb walked steadily on. 'Wizards are feared and respected in equal measure, I have learned that. And just as the weather may turn stormy in a moment, so that respect can turn to fear. It is how people are.'

In a glade he held up his wand; a pale blue light appeared at its moon end and a blue glow fell across his face as well as touching the trunks and low branches of surrounding trees.

'The ground here feels soft. This spot will do us as well as any for tonight.'

Needing no further encouragement, Temmi and Agna threw down their blankets and climbed into them at once.

'Aren't you going to bed too, Master Nubb?' asked Temmi, watching him sit shadowy and alone on the sloping ground nearby.

'Soon . . . it suits me to sit a while and think.'

Laying down his head it occurred to Temmi that what the wizard said was true, unkind words *do* hurt more than stones. The same thought must have been with Agna.

'Goodnight, Master Nubb,' she said gently. 'And thank you.'

Morning came and the rising sun melted away the unpleasantness of the night before, along with the mist in the hollows. They all felt better with the sun on their faces—and better still once they had eaten the breakfast Ollimun cooked for them, frying freshly gathered mushrooms over a good crackling fire. Then it was time to break camp. Ollimun wiped round the frying-pan with a handful of grass. Agna put out the flames. Then each picked up their bundle. They were ready. Filling his lungs with a deep breath of fresh forest air, Temmi took his first proper steps on their journey. If all went well they would eventually take him to a dragon asleep on a mountain of glittering treasure.

Chapter Four

For four days solid they travelled, going higher and higher into the mountains, clambering up steep slopes of bare rock and passing through ancient pine forests, the only sound to be heard the rat-tat-tat of woodpeckers. The walking was hard but they remained cheerful, Ollimun finding time to hunt out healing plants growing among stumps and crevices; Agna picking flowers and stringing them together as she walked along, humming softly to herself as her fingers worked.

Then on the fifth day they reached a high windswept place, after which the land sloped down to a broad flat valley that ran on and on through miles of pathless forest to a line of snowy mountains in the distance.

The stiff breeze caught Ollimun's cloak and hair.

'See those mountains there?' he said pointing with his wand. Temmi and Agna looked. 'When we cross those we will find Grimskalk's home, and with luck a full moon will guide us there on the last night.'

Agna slipped her hand into her pocket and touched Icicle. Soon the time would come to give it up.

Turning away from the distant mountains, Temmi noticed a broad river snaking its way over the valley floor.

'What river is that?' he asked.

Ollimun didn't need to look to know which river Temmi meant. 'Some call it the Burrwash,' he answered, 'although I've heard it called by a dozen different names on its journey to the sea. That is where we set up camp for the night; we must reach its bank by sundown.'

'It seems a long way away,' sighed Agna wearily.

'And it gets no nearer simply by gawping at it. Come on, you two, careful you don't stumble.'

With groans they set off again, downwards this

time, into the broadleaf forest. It was cooler here with many rushing streams where they could pause to drink or wet their faces. This was the only time Ollimun allowed them to stop. Later he gave them nuts and dried fruit to keep up their strength and spirits, but he always made them eat as they went along.

'I never said it would be easy,' he said before anyone thought to complain.

They reached the Burrwash just as the sun was setting in a blaze of blood-coloured light. The river was fast, pebbly and shallow. Seeing it, Agna longed to kick off her boots and run straight into it without a thought to anything else except the blisters on her feet, but Ollimun was already giving out jobs to do. A shelter had to be made, a fire built . . . Temmi went fishing and landed four gleaming brown trout. He showed them to the wizard hoping to impress him, but Ollimun just sniffed and said, 'They'll do.'

Only after the work was done did Ollimun allow anyone to sit by the fire. The fish spat and sizzled; they were done in no time, and with their skins scorched and crispy they tasted altogether so good that what was the point of manners when chins could get greasy and mouths could be stuffed so full that no one could talk even if they wanted to. Beyond the fire's pleasant glow, day faded into velvet night, bats flitting over the river, catching insects.

Temmi, dreamily content, pulled a final fishbone from his mouth and added it to a pile of bones at his side. The long trek forgotten, he half closed his eyes and imagined that he and Agna were on holiday together and that Ollimun was the large shaggy uncle who had taken them along (although this last part took a great deal more imagination— especially now as Ollimun was busily taking a large pinch of snuff, snorting at it like an old badger).

Agna was lost in thoughts of her own. She polished Icicle on her sleeve. Who would have thought that such a tiny thing as this could be the cause of so much tr—

Then she froze—listening—Temmi wide eyed beside her. Ollimun, now half risen from his place, tilted his head, a scowl spreading across his face and his snuffbox lying in the grass. Without a word he flew forward and stamped out the fire, sparks flying wildly in every direction.

Darkness—and now not so pleasant; the smell of wood smoke rising from the last glow of the ashes.

Perhaps it was a trick of their ears but the sound they had heard seemed somehow louder as it reached them again, in the dark.

'What is it?' whispered Agna.

'*Goblins,*' shot back the wizard's voice at once, and a shudder ran down Temmi's spine.

The rumble of goblin war-drums sounded in the distance. Many miles away, probably, thought Temmi, but he felt no better because of it. The drumming was fast and savage; and if in their wildness a stick broke here or a drumskin split there, well, no matter—it was clear that a hundred other drummers were there to hammer on with the noise.

Agna drew in her breath.

'Wizard, I saw something move—in the bushes. *There's something there!*'

Grimly Ollimun pushed them behind him and pointed with the sun end of his wand which fizzled and crackled like a lit firework ready to explode.

He spoke in a loud booming voice.

'Creature, whoever or whatever you are I command you to step out and show yourself.'

Branches trembled. Slowly they parted. Temmi peered more closely as something with a wet quivering nose came crawling into view. A laugh caught in his throat.

'Cush?' he called. 'Is that you, boy?'

Sheepishly the winged bear wagged his stumpy tail.

Chapter Five

Temmi dashed forward, Agna only a few steps behind, but it was right that Temmi should throw his arms around the flying bear first.

'Clever old Cush,' he laughed. 'Were you following us all the time?'

'He must have been,' said Agna. 'But I expect the goblin drums gave him such a fright that he wanted to get closer to our fire.'

'Good job he came too,' said Temmi. 'With so many goblins about he'll make a perfect watchdog. Won't you, Cush? . . . Cush?'

But Cush was having none of it. With a wide yawn he laid his head on his paws and went to sleep.

'The bear has the most sensible idea,' said Ollimun. '*Sleep*. We need to start first thing tomorrow. Oh, listen to those confounded drums, will they never stop?'

With no bracken or moss to soften them, their beds that night were made on hard earth, beneath a lean-to of branches which left little spare room for anyone. Temmi found himself jammed up against the wizard's back, unable to turn over. Still, as uncomfortable as this was, he was so tired he would have slept soundly had it not been for the war-drums going on and on even though midnight was long past. Somehow the dull throbbing worked its way into his head, so when he awoke the next morning it was with a terrible headache.

He shivered beneath his cloak; a cold mist had risen in the night. Down at the river he heard Ollimun washing his face, splashing it with icy water. Then, when the wizard returned, his beard hung with drips, it was time to pick up their things and go: the mist giving perfect cover for sneaking away unseen should goblin eyes be turned in their direction.

'At least the drums have stopped,' said Agna trying to think of something cheerful to say because the clinging mist and deep silence made their mood quite gloomy.

Ollimun picked up his wand and looked around the camp one last time. 'Yes, for the moment,' he said softly. 'But the goblins come as bad news. To be frank, I did not expect them to be quite so close to the Overworld this soon. It worries me. I fear if we do not make it to Grimskalk's mountain by the next full moon it will be too late.'

Hearing this, Temmi promised himself to make each of his strides just that little bit longer.

Without a scrap of breakfast inside them they followed the Burrwash up river for a while, determined to put as many miles between themselves and the goblins as possible. Then, as the sun grew stronger and began to melt away the mist, they slipped under cover of the riverside forest. Cush followed, flitting from branch to branch, stretching out his wings to warm in the watery beams of light. The others went in silence and if they always kept to the shadows it was for a very good reason. It is well known that goblins are cowardly fighters. Rather than meet an enemy face to face, they prefer to dig pits to trap them, or wait to ambush them by the wayside. Temmi looked around. Plenty of bushes and trees gave a hundred good places from which to leap out and attack, the leaves the same colour as goblin skin.

But as the morning went on and they met

neither goblin nor any signs of goblins being near, Temmi started to relax a little. Stretching up he playfully tugged Cush's tail as the flying bear hovered over him. Perhaps the day was not going to be so bad after all.

As he thought this he heard Agna mutter to herself, crossly telling herself off.

She stopped dead and he and Ollimun both turned back to face her.

'What is it?' asked Temmi. 'What's wrong?'

Agna was all the time pushing her hands into her pockets, growing more and more desperate.

'It's Icicle. It's not where I put it. It's disappeared!'

'Are you quite sure?' asked Ollimun gravely.

Agna turned her pockets inside out.

'Look on the ground,' said Temmi.

They searched around them, carefully going over their last few steps. When it became clear that Icicle would not be found so easily, they sat on a log to decide what was to be done about it.

Ollimun closed his eyes and tilted back his head. 'Think carefully now, Agna. When did you last check you had Icicle about you?'

Agna bit her bottom lip. 'I remember it being in my pocket before we set off this morning. I made sure it was good and safe . . . Well, so I thought,' she said lamely. 'Then I knelt down to stroke Cush . . . '

Hearing his name, Cush padded over; he pushed his head beneath one of her hands but Agna didn't even glance up.

'Do you think it fell out there?' she asked. 'Is that where I lost it?'

'You must have done,' said Temmi, his voice dry and cracked with disappointment. 'Just our luck.'

Agna was close to tears. 'I'm so s-sorry. This is all my fault. I should have been more careful.'

Wearily Ollimun pulled himself up by his wand. 'We cannot change what has happened, child. We can only hope to put it right.'

'What! Are you saying we have to go all the way back?' cried Temmi. He couldn't help it, but at that moment he felt furious with Agna. Furious at her carelessness, furious at her waste of valuable time, and furious at the thought of all those unnecessary miles that needed to be trod. But then, when he saw her looking so small and sad and crumpled, his anger left him at once.

'Come on, I'm sure we can find it,' he said dragging her to her feet; and taking her hand in his they started the long journey back.

The sun was halfway up in the sky when they

left the forest and began along the river, sometimes meeting their own footprints in the mud. Agna kept searching her pockets. She was convinced Icicle was in some deep dark corner and she refused to give up until it was found. Cush hovered close to Temmi. He wondered why everyone had a long face. There were no tickles or friendly pats for him now, even when he brushed Temmi's side with the tip of his wing, which usually made him laugh.

'Stop it, Cush. Go away,' snapped Temmi. He was in no mood for Cush's play. 'Let go of my sleeve I tell you, or—'

Lifting his eyes, Temmi suddenly realized this was not one of Cush's rough and tumble games. The flying bear was trying to warn him, and not a moment too soon. There in the distance where their camp had been, Temmi spotted a band of odd-looking creatures. Small and green like poisonous children.

'Goblins!' he uttered. 'Everyone down!'

Snatching Cush from the air, Temmi rolled over and over in the grass with him, before crawling across on their bellies to where Ollimun and Agna lay. Temmi saw that Ollimun had taken a strange wizardly object from his pocket—a tube of metal with a round window at each end. He put it to his sun eye and pushed Cush away as he tried to sniff it.

'What on earth is that?' asked Temmi, in his own way as curious as Cush.

'Hmm . . . ? This? Well, some will call it a fetch-sight or stretch-eye; some say it is a spyglass, and some will know it as a telescope. Here, you have a turn. Close one eye and look through the glass with your other one.'

Temmi did and gave an instant yell.

'*Ollimun—a goblin!* It was here! Its head popped up right in front of me. I could have reached out and touched it with my hand.'

'Take another look, boy. It's perfectly safe. Nothing will bite you. You can spy on the goblins for as long as you like, they will never know.'

Cautiously Temmi lifted the stretch-eye and peered down it again. This time he did not cry out. Keeping it steady he watched the scene before him, as interested in it as anyone who has never before seen a goblin could be (let alone a whole war-party like this!).

Small, crooked, and as green as sour plums, each goblin had pointed ears, many sharp teeth, and a nose as long and bent as an old nail. They wore scraps of rusty armour stolen from the battlefields of others then cut down and shaped to goblin size. Their large feet, too broad for boots, kicked up a great deal of dust; and in the air they excitedly waved spears and knobbly clubs, although some carried nets and those that gave the orders had ancient swords at their sides. Like the armour, these swords were stolen from dead men, then their blades left to rust. How typically cruel of the goblins that they made sure even the smallest cut would poison their enemies' blood.

At a distance Temmi was unable to hear what the goblins said to each other, but through the stretch-eye he saw their mouths move in ugly biting snaps like wolves squabbling for a place at a kill.

They crawled over the spot where the camp had been, some dropping on all fours to sniff the ashes of the fire, no better than dogs; others at the riverside pointing at footprints. And, as Temmi continued to watch, his attention was caught by one particular goblin, a fellow with a bloated body and thin spindly legs. He wore a red lizard-skin jerkin under a ragged piece of chainmail; and around his neck was a bone on a string. Yet it wasn't what he was wearing that caught Temmi's eye, it was the way he was behaving.

For while the other goblins were busy rushing about, snarling and bickering, Red Jerkin stood

absolutely still, staring down into the long grass with a lop-sided grin on his face.

Temmi watched him take a sly look around then all at once snatch something up from the ground. Like all goblins he showed what a skilful thief he was, quick to act when taking something not his own. He was sure no other goblin had noticed him; he did not know about Temmi. But Temmi had seen everything as if standing right next to him.

He pulled away the stretch-eye and stared blankly at the others. His face told them the news was bad.

'Well?' demanded Ollimun.

'Icicle—' whispered Temmi. 'He's got Icicle.'

Chapter Six

Taking turns with the stretch-eye they waited to see what the goblins did next. Temmi felt a horrible churning inside. What if the goblins decided to come swarming after them? After all, their tracks lay fresh and clear in the mud. Ollimun, however, thought this unlikely. He had come across goblins before: he knew their minds well enough to understand their ways.

'Soon they will go back underground,' he said. 'Goblins are so used to darkness that they hate too much sunlight. Besides, when it comes to fighting they are cowards. They prefer to wait in the shadows and they don't have the heart for a long chase.'

As he spoke, Temmi watched the goblins gather in a big group around a particularly ugly general. Two heads taller than any of the others, his shoulders came up to his ears and his arms came down to his knees. A thick ridge of bone made his brow jut out, so his small yellow eyes glowered underneath like two jelly sea-creatures in the shadow of a cliff; and his chin was no less monstrous. To show he was a general, he wore three rats' skulls around his neck. It was a sign of his power and he enjoyed pushing the smaller goblins around, waving his rusty sword at them if they dared to snarl back.

Red Jerkin was there amongst the crowd. He was easy to spot because none of the other goblins wore a jerkin quite the same colour.

'How pleased he looks with himself,' muttered Temmi in disgust, watching him closely through the stretch-eye. 'If only I had my bow and arrows here, then I'd knock that stupid crooked grin off his face for good. Oh, look, Ollimun, they're leaving!'

Agna gave a helpless little groan. 'Icicle will be lost forever and all because of me.'

'What can be lost can be found again,' said Temmi determinedly. 'Come on.'

'Where are you going, boy?' called the wizard after him.

'To rescue Icicle of course, old man. We can't just give up and accept the curse.'

He was right, of course. Preferring not to imagine any of the possible dangers facing them, they followed at a safe distance behind the war-party, hearing the goblins' high screechy voices when the wind changed direction and blew their way.

By what Temmi saw and heard, he soon realized that goblins are an awkward, bad-tempered lot, always finding something to squabble about. In a way they reminded him of the dwarfs, although the dwarfs were never so vicious. And then there was Red Jerkin to watch out for. Soon Temmi and his friends noticed that Red Jerkin had a habit of now and again dropping behind to take a sneaky look at his new-found treasure.

'Foul creature,' muttered Ollimun. 'Look how he slobbers with happiness. He can hardly believe his luck.'

'Let him enjoy it for now,' said Temmi. 'If he keeps going off on his own like that it may give us the chance we need to get it back.'

It was a plan of sorts. For the present, however, they could do nothing more than follow silently behind—and this took no great skill, the goblins were easy to track. Not only did they make a great deal of noise and their big feet kick up clouds of dust, but they spitefully broke branches and trampled flowers. They left a hundred clues showing where they had been and where they were headed. Indeed Temmi found the hardest part about following them was keeping Cush from the air. Poor thing, he did not like walking long distances, yet every time he tried to fly, Temmi was there firmly planting his paws back on the ground. 'Keep low, Cush. Do you want a goblin to spot you?'

But then as evening moved towards night and owls as white as any flying bear started to appear, it became possible for Cush to stretch his wings a little, so long as he stayed close.

'The moon's coming up,' said Agna with a shiver.

She was not the only one to notice. As soon as its first pale beam came over the mountains, the wild drumming started up again. It began with a sudden loud burst and Temmi jumped. The drums sounded so much louder and so much nearer this time that it came as something of a shock to everyone, the noise ambushing them as the goblins themselves might have done.

'Look,' Temmi pointed, 'over there on those hills. I can see fires. *Look—look*, more are springing up all the time!'

They studied the fires, watching them quickly flare. They could make out tiny dark figures dancing around the flames, sometimes leaping through them like mad men.

'They must be the drummers welcoming our goblins back home,' said Agna.

'Now we must keep our wits about us,' said Ollimun, and he explained why. 'The goblins give themselves many front doors, but some are traps. Some are no more than murder-holes leading to bottomless pits.'

He took out his stretch-eye.

'Yes, there they go. Red Jerkin has just gone. Now the drummers. Huh, look how the idiots dance and twirl. The fires are going out! Come on, quickly. Follow me.'

He dashed forward, cloak flying—hair flying; Temmi, Agna, and Cush close on his heels. The hill was carved into ledges with ramps of earth leading to the higher ones. Along each ledge five or six tunnels led away.

'This is the one they went down,' puffed Ollimun at last. He leaned against its side but quickly removed his hand when he found himself sticking to a glob of some rather nasty green goblin slime.

Temmi knelt down and spoke to Cush. 'Now

listen, Cush,' he said firmly. 'This is no place for a bear like you. Not underground. You wait in the forest until we return. No, no. It's no use licking my hand, boy, I won't change my mind. Off you go. Shoo!'

Puzzled, Cush let himself be shoved away. He soared up and circled overhead . . . And when he next looked down he saw that all three humans had gone; blue wand-light fading down the goblin tunnel.

Chapter Seven

The stink of so many large goblin feet that had recently passed that way lingered in the tunnel. Goblin slime glowed and dripped from the walls. 'Don't touch it!' warned Ollimun, but Temmi and Agna didn't need to be told; Temmi sniffing in disgust. Then Agna noticed something else.

'It looks like strange spiky writing with little matchstick pictures instead of letters. What is it, Ollimun?'

'*Goblindy-gook*,' answered the wizard without much interest.

'Can you read what it says?' asked Temmi.

Ollimun shuddered. 'I try not to if it is the usual goblin filth . . . Hello, that's interesting.' He stopped and held his wand-light closer to the graffiti-covered wall. 'Allowing for some dreadful errors, this one reads, "Down with the stranger who makes himself our master". And these say similar things over here . . . Hmm, seems someone is upsetting the little fellows.'

'Good,' said Temmi. 'Anything that makes a goblin's life miserable is fine by me. Come on, let's not fall further behind.'

They went on, the drumming growing more muffled. It seemed to come from below their feet, from deeper underground. Now and again a wild goblin shriek leapt from the darkness like the cry of a ghost; and the air turned steadily colder. Temmi felt goosebumps rising on his arms.

Then Agna realized something. 'I'm sure the sound of drumming's getting louder,' she said in a worried voice.

Temmi instantly forgot the cold. 'The goblins must be coming back!'

'Hold up a moment,' said Ollimun calmly. 'Both of you use your ears.'

They stood still, listening. Several heart-racing minutes went by and as the drumming got neither louder nor fainter it could only mean one thing. The goblin band had come to a halt.

'We'll creep up as close as we can,' said Ollimun. 'And if Red Jerkin is as greedy as I think he is, he'll soon need to sneak off to have another gloat over his treasure. This time we shall be ready for him. This time we shall get Icicle back.'

He sounded so sure that he made Temmi and Agna forget to be afraid. Why, it might even turn out to be easy. Perhaps later they would laugh about it and wonder why they had ever feared the goblins, when in fact they were nothing but empty noise—an endless banging on of drums.

This new confidence carried them further down the tunnel until Ollimun suddenly stopped and turned to them. The drumming sounded very loud. 'I'm sure the goblins are around the next bend,' he said. 'Let your eyes get used to the dark; after that we must feel our way along.'

With these words he tapped his wand gently against the rock and the soft blue light vanished. Temmi took Agna's hand and held it tight, his other hand gripping Ollimun's robe.

It was awkward moving along joined in a line like this, but great care was needed—Ollimun had guessed right, there were indeed goblins around the next bend. At first, however, Temmi hardly noticed them because the tunnel opened into a mighty cavern, its floor littered with boulders the size of houses, and scattered between them lay deep, orange-coloured pools. Grit sparkled in the light of many flickering torches, as Temmi at last turned to the place where the goblins were.

Except for the drummers, most of the war-party were seated on stones around a huge flat rock that acted as a kind of stage in the middle. On it the ugly three-skull general walked up and down impatiently waiting for the drumming to end.

'We'll hide here a while and see what this is all about,' whispered Ollimun.

The drums crashed on, the echo bouncing the horrible noise from every direction. And when the drummers could go no louder or any faster . . . they simply stopped.

Silence.

Temmi's ears rang and the torches spat and crackled. Water dripped from the roof. Moving to the edge of the flat stone, the general began to speak to his men.

'Mutters . . . gripes . . . moans . . . complaints. These what Skinktoe hears. Black words badmouthing our master. A whisper here . . . a whisper there. Ah, but Skinktoe hears. He knows if every word was a lick of one of your treacherous tongues it would wash every raddled, one-eyed tom-cat out ratting in the tunnels. And I here say he who speaks this way about our master speaks nothing less than treason!'

Angry mutters ran through the crowd. The tall goblin held up his hands for silence.

'And I, Skinktoe, say to you it will end. Tongues that creak like rusty gates will be oiled—with *boiling oil*. And stop too your withering looks, uncurl your lips, unsnarl your jaws. Remember who is top dog in this troop. Remember who is your skull-gaffer. I wear three skulls on my chest while some of you cankerpots haven't a tin button to hold up your pants. What I say goes as law—just as what our master says is law to all goblins. And him that says not, let him step here and spit in my eye!'

The mutters grew more excited, rising to a squeal when a squat powerful looking goblin leapt up on to the flat rock and spat on the ground before Skinktoe.

'Stagdog—I might have guessed you,' snarled Skinktoe.

'Me, general. Yes.' Stagdog smiled crookedly. 'And I say down with you and down with the master who plays the big rat over us little mice.'

The two goblins faced each other, and as they did, the watching rabble was beside itself with wild excitement. Every goblin knew there could be no going back. No stepping down. The stage was set for a fight. And as is the goblin way, it started with a round of insults, Skinktoe making sure he began it.

'Why, Stagdog, you dare stand before me. You shadowless creeping lizard. You bit no dog would lick.'

'Fine words, Skinktoe. Did you learn them on the knee of your ape mother?' retorted Stagdog.

Skinktoe shrieked.

Stagdog shrieked even louder.

'You toad jelly!'

'You stench-a-bed!'

'Yesterday's troll bug!'

'Mouldy scrape of teeth slime!'

'Wormcake!'

'Pick-a-wart!'

'Licker-spit!'

'Fill-his-pants!'

'Puke-over!'

'My,' sighed Ollimun from the safety of their hiding place, 'is there anything more charming than a goblin in a temper?'

'They're drawing swords,' said Temmi excitedly. 'There's going to be a proper fight.'

Instantly the goblin rabble was up on its feet, a roar from every throat. For a moment the sound drowned out the drummers who had struck up again, whipping up the crowd's excitement.

The goblins jostled each other like a pack of baboons—Stagdog everyone's favourite.

'Make a maggot house out of him, Stagdog!'

'Give him a mouth in his belly so he grins out his innards!'

'And look,' said Temmi noticing something else. 'There goes Red Jerkin, slipping away like you said he would, Ollimun.'

Agna watched him scornfully. 'He's almost skipping at his own cleverness,' she said. 'He thinks no one has noticed him go.'

'Well,' said Ollimun, 'he can skip to *our* tune in a minute. Now as for us, these great boulders lying about will give all the cover we need, while those awful drums mean we don't have to worry too much about making any noise. So come on, let's close the gap a little on our friend.'

The shrieks of goblins rolled around the cavern, so that the clash of swords was only faintly heard. However, Temmi and his friends had other matters to worry about than how the fight was going, and if one of them did pop their head up it was only for the latest sighting of the goblin in the red jerkin.

'There seems to have been an old rockslide over there,' reported Temmi. 'I'm sure that's where he's headed. If he goes the other side of it he'll be completely hidden from view.'

Temmi had guessed right. Red Jerkin disappeared behind the heap of broken rock and didn't reappear. Reaching the foot of it, Ollimun rolled back his sleeves.

'I'm going to climb to the top,' he told Temmi and Agna. 'Don't worry, the shadows are deep enough to hide me. You two wait here. When I give the signal go behind and get Icicle.'

'What about Red Jerkin?' asked Agna.

'Safely dealt with. I shall put him into an enchanted sleep. Right, off I go. Remember to keep watching out for my sign.'

'Be as quick as you can, wizard,' pleaded Agna. Now she and Temmi had nothing to do but wait, the constant crashing of drums and the goblins' mindless howls made them both uneasy. The contest between Skinktoe and Stagdog was not yet settled and their rusty blades sliced the air and sparked against rock. How good it would be, thought Temmi, to get Icicle then slip quietly away, leaving behind the goblins and their messy business for good.

'Look,' said Agna, her nails digging into his

arm. 'Ollimun is lowering his wand. I hope he gives that thieving goblin a good sharp prod.'

'It's a wand, Agna, not a harpoon. All Ollimun has to do is touch the goblin and he is asleep. Yes—see, he's pulling it back. He's waving to us. Come on, that's our signal to go.'

Behind the rockfall it was so dark it was difficult to see. Ollimun's voice came floating down. 'I daren't risk giving you a light. Use my voice to guide you. Have you found him yet?'

'Yes,' replied Temmi sourly. 'I tripped over his big feet.' Glancing up he could just make out the tip of the wizard's beard hanging down. Agna dropped onto her hands and knees.

She bobbed back up almost immediately.

'Temmi, I've got it! I've got Icicle!'

'Well done,' he said grinning with relief.

'Before we leave there is one more thing,' came Ollimun's voice instructing them. 'I'm going to lower a small jar of ointment. Rub a little under Red Jerkin's nose. It will make him forget about Icicle, so when he wakes up he won't raise the alarm. Be careful, mind, it's strong magic. If you breath in the fumes you'll become forgetful too.'

Something came out of the gloom on a length of string, brushing against Temmi's shoulder. He took the jar off the end, already wincing at the idea of having to touch the goblin's slimy green skin.

'Why do I always end up doing the worst jobs?' he complained.

'Because I used to be a princess,' said Agna loftily. 'Now be quick, for goodness' sake.'

Temmi opened the jar, and ignoring the wizard's warning, breathed in some of the fumes. 'Umm . . . what *was* I supposed to do with this?' he asked.

Agna sighed and reminded him. Temmi shook his head clear of forgetfulness and quickly smeared a little ointment under the goblin's nose.

'Good work,' came down Ollimun's delighted voice, hearing the jar's lid click back on. 'Now, the sooner we're away from this dreary goblin-infested place the better. I'll meet you on the other side.'

Back together and with Icicle safe in Agna's pocket, they had just begun to creep away when a tremendous roar ripped through the cavern like an explosion and the drummers went into a frenzy, beating their drums as if they meant to smash them into tiny pieces.

'What is it?' asked Agna worriedly. 'What's happened?'

'I expect that old goblin fight has come to an

end,' said Temmi. 'Not that it bothers me who's won, so long as it means there is one less goblin in the world.'

But Temmi was more interested than he pretended. In the silence following the great noise he listened to hear which of the two goblins spoke.

It was Stagdog.

He gasped for breath, his throat dry and his voice harsh.

'*There* as it should be . . . Skinktoe—meat for worms . . . And we here agree . . . No stranger shall be our master.'

'Tell us then, Stagdog, what do we do to get rid of him?' called a voice from the uneasy buzz arising on all sides.

'We do nothing. *Nothing*, you hear. We wait until the time is right.'

'And what do we say when the master asks about Skinktoe?'

'Leave that to me to make smooth. A few of you throw Skinktoe's body in a corner and heap it up with stones. But first give me his rat skulls . . . There's handsome, three squeakers in a row. Now the little general's cutter. Good—good . . . '

However, before he could admire himself as well as he thought he deserved, Stagdog gave a short

66

piercing scream. 'That creature over there. What is it? What is it? It looks like a bear with feathers!'

His words went through Temmi like a spear. *A bear with feathers*—it could mean only one thing . . . 'Oh no,' he uttered. 'Cush has only gone and followed us down here.'

Chapter Eight

Everything was starting to go wrong—horribly wrong; and it was about to get a great deal worse. Temmi felt a shout of rage building up inside him like a volcano about to blow. He wanted to shout a warning to Cush—he wanted to roar at the goblins and frighten them so badly that they'd leave the young bear alone. He wanted to do something—*anything*—rather than stand by and do nothing at all. Guessing this, Ollimun shot his hand over Temmi's mouth and bundled him onto the ground. He knew Temmi would be furious with him—but better this than have him do something stupid he might regret later.

Across on the other side of the cavern the

goblins were even more confused as to what they should do: they had never seen a flying bear before. Some went pale (yellow, actually), some were snarling fierce, some chanted, 'Kill it! Kill it! Kill the beast!'

Every slack and crooked mouth was bawling—making a noise although not necessarily making sense.

Then Temmi heard Stagdog scream louder than anyone else, and take control.

'Enough! Quiet, you rattle mouths. *Quiet!* Good, now listen to me. If we get the ambush nets, we can catch us the beast. Then think of the fine time we'll have pulling out its feathers and making it howl.'

A roar of cruel delight went up. Temmi fought free of Ollimun's grasp.

'Let go of me, wizard! I have to see what they're doing.'

He rushed to join Agna who was peering around a boulder.

'I can hardly bear to watch,' she said, a tremble in her voice. 'Those evil goblins have got nets. Poor Cush. He's growling and his fur is standing on end, but I know he's frightened. Oh . . . they're throwing the nets . . . They've got him! Cush is all caught up.'

Temmi watched in silence. His glare was fierce but his eyes glistened with tears. Cush, trapped in the goblins' nets, rolled about getting more and more tangled. The goblins danced around him, tormenting him in every way. They waved their torches in his face, they prodded and pinched him through the nets, they tried to pluck feathers from his snowy wings. Cush barked, sending them scattering, but each time the goblins came crowding back again, screaming and laughing.

And as Temmi's sorrow for Cush grew, so did his hatred of Stagdog. It boiled inside him. The goblin had jumped up on to a rock where he could be seen and heard by his men. At his shrill command twenty goblins swarmed forward and lifted Cush off the ground. Cush whimpered and Stagdog leapt down and danced wildly before him.

'Stagdog is braver than Skinktoe! Stagdog is braver than a wild bear!' he yelled boastfully.

'The bully,' said Agna with feeling. 'Cush isn't much more than a baby.'

Watching the scene closely moment by moment, Temmi and the others had unwisely forgotten about another danger much nearer to them—Red Jerkin, whose enchanted sleep was coming to an end.

With a snort his eyes flickered open, his head full of strange dreams. His long lizard-like tongue licked his top lip. It felt strangely sticky—well, stickier than usual—and tasted odd too. He could hear a lot of noise and as he clawed his way unsteadily to his feet, he spotted Temmi and the others. Now, he might have forgotten all about Icicle but this was something altogether different. At once he began to shriek in a high-pitched voice.

'Spies! Spies! Spies in the tunnels!'

In one movement Ollimun spun round and pointed. Lightning sprang from his wand and struck Red Jerkin's arm. This only made him howl louder.

And despite the commotion there was something urgent in his voice that soon attracted Stagdog's attention.

'What say it? Spies? Spies in the tunnels? Brothers, bring more nets and be snap about it.'

'Time to show ourselves,' said Ollimun gravely. And they stepped out from their hiding place.

Agna gave a gasp seeing the wide sea of goblin faces rushing towards them. She took a step back; Temmi grabbed her arm and pulled her next to him. 'Stay together, Agna,' he told her firmly.

The goblins gripped their nets ready to throw

them. Yet the battle was not all one sided. Again and again Ollimun pointed his wand and it flashed and scorched many a goblin there; and they howled far louder than their little wounds deserved. But in the end there were simply too many goblins to hold back and their stinking nets fell over them. Before they could be clawed off, more nets came flying through the air and the three friends were trapped as neatly as in a spider's web. From there it took no more than a sharp tug to have them off their feet and a few seconds more to see them tied up. How the goblins enjoyed that, pulling the ropes as tightly as they could.

They peered in at their miserable prisoners.

'Stagdog—Stagdog!' A cross-eyed goblin started to get very excited. 'This conjuring man, I know him. He scorched my cousin's nose under Blunt Tooth mountain. Those of us with straight eyes should watch him.'

'Pah—he's nothing without his stick,' said Stagdog scornfully. When the fighting was fiercest he had been at the back urging his men on, now he came forward, crawling over their heads to get to the front. His grin appeared at the nets, and reaching through he snatched Ollimun's wand. A mistake, as it happened. The wand immediately flew up and thwacked him hard around the ears. Never did a grin vanish so quickly.

'Tell the stick to behave, conjurer. Tell it! Or let it be splinters for our fires.'

Reluctantly Ollimun gave the command and the wand came floating down into Stagdog's hand. His fingers clutched it up.

'What a prize,' he gloated. 'What a trophy.' He held the wand high above his head. 'Skinktoe, bears, and conjurers—Stagdog more mighty than them all!'

Bundled up and mocked, Temmi, Ollimun, Agna, and Cush were carried head high by the goblins, deeper underground. Cush chewed his ropes but it was quite useless. And everywhere Temmi looked goblins swarmed like cockroaches, their drums echoing off the solid walls.

It was like a nightmare—but one with no chance of waking up and escaping from. The ropes pulled tightly across Temmi's chest. He found it hard to breathe. Next to him he felt Agna tremble.

'Don't worry, Agna,' he whispered. 'We'll get out of this.'

Yet it was hard to see how—and if they did

would they ever find their way back to the surface—to open skies and sunshine? Temmi was determined to remember each twist and turn of the tunnel, but in the end had to admit defeat—it unwound before them like a ball of wool, a dozen different passageways leading off left and right.

Then came journey's end. Temmi saw it was a cavern much grander than the one where they had been captured: this one was large enough to swallow a town. Around its edges were the goblins' caves, each protected by a stout metal door to keep out thieves and neighbours (which for goblins were the same thing).

Hearing the drums of the returning war-party, the stay-at-home goblins turned out to greet it. They rushed from their caves (locking them afterwards) or left their places by the great fires which were dotted throughout the cavern. Old goblins—like green skeletons in ridiculous ragged turbans—dragged themselves out of bubbling slime pools where they bathed. Young goblins (called *Stenchlings* and for a very good reason) brought along their pet spitting-toads (which were rather like big glum-faced dolls) holding them up and squeezing them so that the vile creatures lived up to their name. Then after a while the stenchlings grew braver and came creeping closer . . .

'Oh, for ten minutes with my wand,' moaned Ollimun as crooked fingers reached up to pull his beard, nimbly stripping it of the glass beads that were threaded there.

However, most scorn was directed at Cush.

'Look at the flying bogle!' squawked the stenchlings. 'Try to make it growl. Try to make it growl!'

Taking advantage of the crowds, Stagdog urgently beckoned his wife across and handed her the wand and Skinktoe's sword. She nodded knowing they had to be hidden away in their cave for safe keeping. She wiped her hands before she took the wand. What a marvellous treasure to have! They swapped grins and she was gone.

As she disappeared, the drums suddenly stopped and the procession came to a halt. The nets were thrown down and the prisoners inside them were surrounded—by armed guards on three sides, and a long narrow flight of steps on the fourth side. The steps led to a stone chair; on it, high above the fires, sat a shadowy figure, his hands gripping the carved armrests.

'That must be the master who Stagdog hates so much,' whispered Agna.

Temmi rubbed the rope burns on his arm. He had a bad feeling about this.

Stagdog bowed and, for all his brave words earlier, approached the steps like a whipped dog.

'Where is Skinktoe?' demanded the figure at the top, his voice as friendly as a blast of cold air.

'Dead, master,' answered Stagdog. 'There was a great battle in the Overworld. Skinktoe took a spike, it was a black hour.'

'But I see you managed to rescue his skulls,' said the voice drily.

'It was a cruel bitter battle, master. The men needed a general. Many were killed. But see, I have brought prisoners to please you.'

'Let me see them *properly*.'

'Hurry—hurry,' growled Stagdog as his men tipped out all the nets except Cush's. The prisoners got up slowly. Temmi had his knife snatched from his belt—but Agna felt Icicle safe in her boot where she had managed to tuck it. All three blinked in the torchlight.

A long silence followed, broken only by the crackle of flames or the bump of a settling log. Temmi heard his own heart thudding.

'H-has Stagdog not pleased his master?' The goblin grinned nervously, his voice whingeing and fearful.

'Oh, Stagdog, you have pleased me more than you can ever know.'

The shadowy figure rose, and something that had lain hidden at his feet rose with him. Slowly they began to come down into the light.

Temmi stared.

'I don't believe it,' he heard Agna whisper. 'It's not possible . . . ' His own mouth fell open but no sound came out. He could see now there was no mistake.

Tin Nose.

It was Tin Nose.

And close beside him, as large and terrifying as ever—Frostbite his wolf.

Chapter Nine

Tin Nose was dressed in long robes as soft and grey as shadows; around his head a tight circle of red goblin gold, and in place of his real nose, which had been bitten off long ago when Frostbite was a cub, he wore a replacement chosen from his collection of false ones. It was pointed and silver with a line of river pearls running down its ridge, which gave him the appearance of a fierce bird of prey. His skin was no longer blue with cold (as Temmi remembered) but grey from lack of sunlight. Frostbite by his side was every bit as dangerous as ever he was; a heavy lead collar clamped around his neck.

Halfway down the steps Tin Nose stopped. He was almost amused by their expressions.

'You stare in disbelief. Can it be you think I am some kind of ghost?'

Temmi could hardly speak, hardly get out a word, but as silence wouldn't do he forced himself.

'But . . . last time I saw you, you fell into the chasm. You dropped onto the rocks below. Your bones should have been broken into a hundred pieces.'

'I fell onto snow, boy, and lived—as did Frostbite. The Cold has always served us well.' He glared meaningfully at Agna.

'The goblins found him there,' spoke up Stagdog. 'He made himself our—' He winced. 'That is, we goblins made him our master.'

'Lord of the goblins,' said Tin Nose distastefully. 'Living in a goblin hole instead of returning home to the lands of snow and ice.' He smiled grimly. 'For how could I go home? I was defeated, there would be nothing for me there but shame. But now, now things are different. They are turned around. You have fallen into my hands and my shame is ended. Frostbite and I are free to return to our homelands in triumph and you our enemies will be dragged along behind us like dogs. And once we are there you will both stand trial for treason, for you brought fire and warmth to the High Witchlands. *You* betrayed the Cold.'

Frostbite growled as if agreeing. He hated the darkness and the goblins' warmth-giving fires as much as his master did.

Tin Nose's gaze then took in Ollimun.

'You have fallen in with new company, I see. A wizard. Stagdog, tell me, where is his wand?'

'His stick, master? Why, Stagdog nashed it. He nashed it in battle. He did it with his cutter, master, before the conjurer was netted.'

Stagdog shot Temmi and the others a sharp look, warning them to keep their mouths shut. One way or another he meant to keep Ollimun's wand for himself.

'Is this the truth, Stagdog?' Tin Nose turned to him abruptly. 'I warn you, goblin, my wolf has developed a real taste for fresh green meat, so if you are telling lies . . . ' And he hissed, 'They must not escape me a second time, do you understand?'

'It's the truth, master,' whined the goblin. 'Stagdog would not dare trick you. You know how he dances a shiver at the great wolf's song.'

'Very well, I suppose you are right. Put the prisoners in the cells—that bear creature with them. Tomorrow at first light we set off for the High Witchlands.'

With this command he turned and made his

way back up to his stone chair, Frostbite's sleek fur at his heels. The others, meanwhile, were quickly surrounded by goblins and jostled to some dark caves behind the steps. Each cave had a door made of iron bars. Behind some were goblin lawbreakers—thin poor things—who stared up gloomily at the latest arrivals.

Stagdog waved a key that was shaped more like a spiked club. The door to an empty cell was flung open and the prisoners shoved inside. Then the door clanged shut and was locked; Stagdog flashing a final toothy grin through the bars before hurrying away.

Cautiously Ollimun moved to the door to check the passageway was empty. 'Thank goodness he's gone,' he said. 'Is everyone all right? And Icicle—is it safe?'

Agna nodded and Temmi crouched down to free Cush who was still caught up in nets.

'The troubles you get us into, boy,' he said, but not crossly: he could not be cross with Cush after the goblins had treated him so badly.

Cush shook himself free of the final net and gave a sad wag of his tail.

Finding that nobody was hurt beyond a graze or two, it was then time to make a thorough search of their cell. This took no more than a minute. The cell didn't go back very deep into the rock and had no windows, of course. Temmi shook the metal door.

'Solid,' he said. He rested his head against the cold bars and sighed. 'If only you had somehow managed to hold on to your wand, Ollimun,' he said, wishing aloud. 'Then we'd be out of here in no time.'

'If a wand is all we need, I must see what I can do about getting mine back,' said Ollimun sounding surprisingly jaunty. 'That goblin, Stagdog, kind fellow—he's taking care of it for me.'

'What? You really think you *can* get it back?' asked Agna eagerly.

Ollimun smiled. 'The bond that joins a wizard and his wand is as strong as the bond that joins a boy and his bear. Why do you think Tin Nose was so anxious to know where my wand had disappeared to? He knew if it was nearby it would certainly find its way back to me. Poor, dim Stagdog doesn't understand. I think he may regret trying to keep us apart. It will be his lesson for calling me a conjurer and my wand a stick.'

Suddenly Temmi felt his gloom pushed aside like a heavy black curtain and *hey presto* there was sunshine.

'What are you going to do?' he asked.

'Nothing this very minute. But once the goblins are safely asleep—' The wizard rubbed his hands gleefully. '—there may be a little magic in the air.'

So they waited, listening out for some sort of sign that the goblins were settling down. And what better sign was it than when the drums finally stopped. The goblin prisoners on either side gave a deep sigh, lay down on their hard floors, and went to sleep.

Ollimun held a finger to his lips. 'Time for me to go to work,' he told Agna and Temmi before sitting cross-legged before them.

'Can we do anything to help?' asked Agna.

'No. This is wizard's work. Cush is safely dozing—good, let him stay that way. I must insist on perfect calm around me. Not a sound, not a movement. Remember that.' And he took several deep breaths, closed his eyes, and called for his wand—not with his voice but with his thoughts, which travel much further.

Agna and Temmi watched, both keeping as still as possible. Temmi imagined his nose itched but didn't dare scratch it—not after Ollimun's warning. Soon his legs ached and his arms felt heavy and he grew tired of catching each breath in case it came out as a sigh. Agna was the same, until from the corner of her eye she caught a movement.

'*Look*.' She pointed at the bars. Temmi leapt back in fright, jumping clear of the long, black snake that had appeared there. Like rats and wild cats, snakes found a ready-made home among the goblins' tunnels. They liked the cool darkness and a fresh goblin or two. Temmi stared in horror; the snake rising up and displaying its fangs. Before it could strike, he flew over to Ollimun and shook his shoulders.

'Wake up!' he cried, because with his eyes closed the wizard looked asleep. 'Wake up before the snake bites you!' He knew he was not supposed to be disturbed, but surely this was different.

Ollimun's eyes flickered open.

'Silly boy,' he said.

Reaching through the bars, he caught the snake by the throat, and before it had time to coil around his arm he dragged it inside the cell . . . and suddenly it grew straight and turned into his wand.

'*Oh*.' Temmi felt rather foolish—but matters were moving swiftly on. Already at its sun end the wand fizzled with a white hot light. Temmi was forced to look away. Ollimun touched the lock and it sprang open with the sound of snapping metal. They were free.

They tumbled out, Cush eagerly shaking off his doze.

'This way!' said Ollimun, his wand in his hand and once again a part of him.

He led them past sleeping prisoners shivering in their cells. He did not know where he was going but one thing was for sure, he did not want to go back into the main part of the cavern, for it needed only one half awake goblin and the alarm was raised. So when they came across a tunnel leading in the opposite direction, they had little other choice than to take it.

For goblins' work the tunnel was unusually wide and straight with no lesser passageways leading off it. Had they time to ask, Ollimun might have told them how it was dug by a much older and more skilful people. But at that moment he had more important matters on his mind. Temmi did not ask what, but he guessed. The tunnel was taking them deeper and deeper into the earth. To make matters worse they soon had to go in complete darkness, feeling their way blindly along the glass-smooth walls. And if Temmi was fortunate not to trip over a sleeping goblin on the way, he certainly stumbled over Cush a good many times.

Ollimun tutted and sighed. They were getting nowhere. He risked a pale light from the moon end of his wand, holding it close to the ground. Temmi and Agna stopped clinging to the walls and sprang to his side.

'Keep your pace to a good steady march,' the wizard told them. This they did.

'It just keeps on going down!' wailed Agna a while later.

'But away from the goblins,' said Temmi. 'And it's just too well dug to go to nowhere at all. There must be something at the end.'

He hoped he did not mean a bottomless pit.

Suddenly Agna stopped. She lifted her head, every part of her seeming to listen.

'I can hear a trickling sound,' she said. And she peered down the tunnel with the same concentration. 'I'm sure I can see something moving—glinting.'

'A river maybe?' suggested Temmi hopefully.

'Of course—*a river*,' cried Ollimun. The brightness in his voice died abruptly. He groaned. 'Oh no, not so soon.'

Behind them, like the heart of the Underworld coming alive, the goblin drums had begun their familiar pounding. Their escape had been discovered!

Chapter Ten

Temmi's and Agna's young legs were much faster than Ollimun's. The two youngsters raced ahead with Cush so by the time the wizard reached the stone river wall, they had untied the first war-canoe and were waiting for him.

'Hurry up, Ollimun!' urged Temmi holding the rope; Agna and Cush already on board.

'Give . . . me . . . a . . . moment.' Ollimun bent over, struggling to get back his breath, his hair in his eyes and his beard over one shoulder. Then taking control of himself he straightened and pointed his wand.

An orange flash sprang from it, spreading fire amongst the other, empty canoes. Hungry flames crackled and jostled each other, and firelight fanned out over the river, blood red and streaked with yellow.

'That should stop them following us.'

Content with his magic, Ollimun clambered down into the canoe, and once Temmi had tossed aboard the mooring rope, he leapt in after him.

The canoe was little more than a hollowed-out log with a fierce goblin-carving at the front and a tail spiky with nails rising at the back. Paddles lay in the bottom—three of which were immediately seized.

Everyone did their bit, paddling the canoe out into the middle of the river. They felt the strong smooth current catch them; they felt the canoe pick up speed and flow with it. After that they let the river do all the hard work, using a paddle now and again to keep themselves on a steady course.

Only then did Temmi dare risk looking back. He saw how fiercely the fires burned, seeing, too, little angry figures dancing with rage, black against the orange flames. He laughed. Then the river swept round a bend and the light was gone.

'Allow me,' said Ollimun, driving back the darkness with light from the blazing sun-tipped end of his wand.

'That's better,' said Agna. 'Not that it tells us anything useful like where we might be going. Do you know, Ollimun?'

'No—that will very much depend on what river this is. I must say it doesn't seem right not knowing a river's name. It feels impolite, I like to be properly introduced.'

Introduced to a river, thought Temmi. He smiled to himself, wizards have the oddest notions . . .

Meanwhile the river flowed powerfully on. As far as Temmi could judge they travelled at a considerable speed, whirling eddies breaking out around them, strings of bubbles trapped under the surface unable to rise. Nor was the water always smooth: dips and hollows had to be ridden up and down, and foam flew over the ugly carving at the front.

For most of the time the walls upon either side rose smoothly from the water's edge, meeting in a rough arch, high and unseen in the darkness overhead. However, occasionally, they visited vast caverns with stalagmite pillars, where cold mountain water dripped off the roof in a steady rain.

With so much water and so much movement it was not surprising that the noise of the two together could prove deafening. When it did, it was useless trying to talk: the best any of them could do was sit tight and wait for a calmer stretch, which usually appeared around the next bend.

All of them were wet through. Wet and cold. Only Cush didn't mind. Hanging his head over the front of the canoe, he let the river breeze ruffle his fur, enjoying himself as much as if he were flying. Then Temmi noticed him lift his head, his nose quivering as he sniffed the air.

'Cush . . . What is it?'

Wurrr. Cush broke into a suspicious snarl. His small dark eyes stared steadily back the way they had come. Ollimun turned to see what bothered him so.

'By all the planets!' he cried. 'Lights. I fear we may have goblins on our tail.'

'How *can* they be?' asked Temmi.

'They must have had other canoes further up river.'

'And they're bound to catch us,' added Agna. 'Think of all those extra pairs of hands busy with a paddle.'

Temmi had an idea. While Ollimun and Agna grabbed paddles themselves and began to shovel water for all they were worth, he took the loose end of the rope (the one that had been secured to the river wall) and tied it around Cush's middle.

91

Cush turned back and watched him curiously, his tongue hanging from the side of his mouth. Temmi gave him a gentle shove.

'Time for you to lend a hand, Cush—or do I mean paw? Or perhaps I mean wing. Oh, never mind—*fly*, boy! Fly the best you can.'

Cush needed no excuse to take to the air. Immediately they felt the canoe jolt as the slack rope tightened and Cush began towing them. The canoe cut the water like a knife, hissing spray flying up into their faces.

Agna and Temmi laughed and called Cush a clever bear and encouraged him every way they could. Ollimun meanwhile took out his stretch-eye and turned it on the approaching goblins, putting the glass up to his moon eye because it saw better in the dim light.

'A couple of war-canoes similar to ours,' he reported. 'I'd say a team of thirty goblins in each . . . Tin Nose there too, that monster of a wolf by his side. My, Tin Nose has a face to match the goblin carving. He keeps shouting at his crew. I expect he's ordering it to paddle faster.'

'Are they still catching us up?' asked Agna worried.

With a snap, Ollimun closed his stretch-eye. 'Afraid they are. Give them another five minutes

and they'll be ready to board us.' He glanced up. 'Temmi, can you manage to get more speed out of Cush?'

Temmi shook his head. 'This is all play to Cush—a game. Besides he's starting to tire.'

'Then,' said Ollimun gravely, 'one way or another I must settle this matter with magic.'

Trying not to rock the boat, he clambered towards the spiky tail at the rear. As he went, Temmi noticed his wand once more glow white hot at its powerful sun end, the garish light strong enough to reveal an entire length of river between two bends.

Broken snatches of drumming sounded clearly now and leaning over the side, Temmi was in time to catch two craft come around the upriver bend and into the light. They approached so fast that their prows lifted clean out of the water, and he could make out the determined grins on the faces of the crews. Tall and silently fuming, Tin Nose stood at the front of his boat, one hand resting on the carved figurehead, the other gripping a drawn sword. Beside him, Frostbite savagely displayed his fangs. And behind them both was Stagdog—stripped of his rat skulls, and forced to sweat over a paddle like a slave.

'Temmi—quickly get Cush on board!' The wizard's call was urgent.

Temmi gave a gentle tug on the rope and Cush glided down and landed at his feet.

'Good, now we are ready,' said Ollimun.

Before either Agna or Temmi could ask *ready for what?*, Ollimun pointed his glowing wand at the solid roof above. A blinding flash was followed by a crack, and a shockwave ran through the air.

And then, quite simply, it rained stones— falling between Temmi's boat and the two goblin craft.

In a similar way that drizzle can sometimes lead to a raging thunderstorm, it began with a scattering of small stones, but quickly grew heavier and the stones much larger. Suddenly great chunks of shattered rock were tumbling down. The river frothed and boiled. But it was far from over. With a boom that nearly knocked Agna off her feet, an avalanche of churning rock came crashing down. It felt like an earthquake. And from out of the dust and spray a single gigantic wave appeared. It rushed at the company, picked up their boat, and after much jolting and shipping of water, set it on its fizzing crest and carried it forward.

'Hang on! Hang on for your very lives!' bellowed Ollimun, but his words were lost in the cold black roar.

Riding the wall-like wave—sometimes just inches short of the roof—they raced on at such speed that Temmi didn't have time to be afraid. As the Underworld flashed by, his lank hair streamed ragged and spray pelted him as hard as grit. An attempt to shout left him choking on a mouthful of water.

Then he saw light.

Daylight.

A moment later they exploded into snow and forest.

The wave stormed up the banks on either side, washing over the top, breaking against trees. Then—swiftly—it began losing power and height.

Chapter Eleven

The dying wave brought the badly listing canoe ashore at the next broad bend. Leaping out, Temmi was surprised to find his legs so shaky that he fell face first into the snow. He lifted his head and blinked at the bright daylight.

'How strange . . . snow in summer,' he said confused.

'Not here, boy,' said Ollimun. 'We have reached the Lands of Snow where spring and summer come together and last only weeks.' He paused. 'Although just at which particular corner of those lands remains to be seen.' Bending over his bundle he took out his warm cloak and put it on. He suggested his young companions changed too. Now was the time to wear the thick winter clothes they had carried for so long—and quickly before they froze. Already Agna's teeth had begun to chatter.

Life was simpler for Cush. With a shake all the loose drips flew off him and he was done. To her dismay, Agna found her new clothes were patched and smelt musty, but she gladly put them on. And feeling much safer as well as much warmer, she took Icicle from her boot, polished it and slipped it back into her pocket.

Temmi was nearly ready too. He did up his last button and stared into the distance. He saw snow and mountains—and it was much the same picture whichever way he turned: the snow unendingly white, and the mountains soaring peaks of ice.

He said, 'If we don't know where we are, how do we know which direction to take?'

'I didn't say I don't know where we are,' replied Ollimun. 'I said it remains to be seen. If you will just stand back and give me room . . . '

He unhooked two leather pouches from his belt, took out the various things they held, and opened both pouches until perfectly flat. Temmi watched in delight. They had unfolded into maps, beautiful and highly detailed maps, lovingly drawn in brown and black ink. Mountains had their names written in runes, and there were forests and rivers marked, and secret passes through or under the mountains, and the best places to find rare herbs and mushrooms, and the criss-crossed paths of birds and beasts when they migrate. Ollimun took out something else—a little windowed box rather like a watch (if Temmi had known what a watch was). He called it a compass. And using that together with the maps and the stretch-eye (which let him study the mountains around) he was able to point to where they were on one of the maps.

'This is us. Here. On the western borders of the High Witchlands. The river may have saved our skins but it's taken us in completely the wrong direction.'

Temmi knelt down in the snow to see better. 'There are lots of mountains. Which one is Grimskalk's?'

The answer made dismal news. Ollimun pointed to a tiny dragon on the *second* map.

Agna stared in disbelief. 'Oh, but that's miles away! We'll never reach it by the next full moon. Not through deep snow!'

Temmi leapt to his feet and snatched up his now much lighter bundle. 'Well, I'm not giving up,' he said stoutly. 'Not now, not until the full moon comes up and shines in my face. And if you are my friends you'll do the same.'

Ollimun silently gathered up his things.

They set off through the snow, making hard work of it because it was so deep, with Cush hovering for much of his time, waiting for them to catch up. This was how it went on until they reached a forest, where snow was heaped upon the trees, but on the ground lay shallow and even. Here they were more able to get into their stride. At midday Cush got hungry and went exploring. Temmi knew he had returned when a fish dropped from the sky and landed at his feet. He picked it up—already it was frozen. He understood this was Cush's way of saying sorry for all the trouble he had caused amongst the goblins.

All through the afternoon they walked on, finding it as dull and tedious to walk through snow as to look at it. Yet they had one reason to be thankful. Goblins hate the cold as much as they hate being away from their dreary holes. 'I doubt we shall meet another living soul in this frozen edge-of-the-world place,' Ollimun told them confidently.

Agna stopped. 'You talk too soon, wizard. Look there—'

Not far off through the trees they saw a figure; his back to them and standing perfectly still.

Temmi reached for his knife but of course the sheath was empty.

'Hide!' whispered Ollimun. 'We'll not show ourselves to this stranger until we are sure of his business.'

He and Temmi dived behind a snowdrift; Agna took cover behind a tree.

'Oh no,' said Temmi. 'What about Cush?'

Temmi might well have called the bear's name just then. For as if in answer, Cush came gliding through the branches: he swept over Temmi's head making straight for the stranger.

'There is something odd in the way the fellow stands so absolutely still,' said Ollimun.

'Well, he better watch out,' said Temmi. 'Here comes Cush.'

Wings spread, the bear flew down and struck the stranger between his shoulders . . . and without so much as a cry of surprise he slowly slumped to the ground.

Agna stepped out from behind her tree.

'Why, it's a snowman,' she laughed.

Ollimun frowned. 'Be that as it may, snowmen do not build themselves. From here on we must proceed with care.'

They did, and soon came across other snowmen—solitary white figures standing amongst the trees. At first it was amusing to meet them. Then, as they kept on cropping up, there seemed something more sinister about them. Temmi couldn't help noticing that they all managed to be facing his way. He shuddered—*watching him*, it appeared. Then he noticed something else— something even *more* shocking.

'That snowman,' he gasped, 'I recognize it. I'm sure we've passed by it once before.'

'I can't see how,' said Ollimun. 'We haven't gone in circles or we'd have met our own footprints.'

Agna gave a brief uneasy laugh. 'And snowmen can't move by themselves . . . can they?'

To settle the matter, Temmi found a stick and carved a deep cross into the snowman's chest.

'Now let's see what happens.'

They pressed on, the snowmen starting to appear in groups of two, three, and even four. Their faces no longer quite so friendly.

This is foolish, thought Temmi. They are only snow, only frozen water; not flesh and blood like real men. Yet still he kept glancing over his shoulder, unable to shake off the feeling that they were being followed.

Then he gave a startled cry.

'The snowman I marked with a cross,' he said pointing. This time it stood with two others— and not a footprint in sight.

'Maybe there are two snowmen with crosses on them,' suggested Agna weakly.

Temmi shook his head vigorously. 'Impossible. That's the same one all right. But now he looks as if he's plotting with the others.'

'I don't like this, I don't like this at all,' said Ollimun. 'I sense bewitchment and it is not of my doing.' His wand started to glow with ready magic—but ready for what? The snowmen might have made them uneasy but they were doing them no harm.

'Let's try walking faster and see what they do,' said Agna.

This they did: keeping together in a close group they marched on determinedly.

The snowmen quickly multiplied. They looked angrier by the minute. Little groups formed soldier ranks with here and there a stick that could be a spear. Unable to resist, Cush swept in low and knocked off a line of heads—but it didn't stop the snowmen's numbers from growing.

'They're getting closer!' cried Temmi.

Ahead, to the sides, and behind—*snowmen*; with yet more coming up through the trees. Nobody saw one move by so much as a snowflake, but seconds later Temmi and the others were surrounded, snowmen standing shoulder to shoulder and many bodies deep.

Then one of the snowmen spoke to them.

'You don't look like goblins, but it doesn't mean we can trust you. Who are you? Tell us what you are doing in the forest. Speak the truth. There are at least three arrows pointing at each of you. They will stick in your hearts if you try anything slippery.'

Staring in the direction of the voice, Agna saw it wasn't a snowman that had spoken at all. It was a boy. And dotted amongst the snowy figures were other youngsters, similarly dressed in fur-trimmed hooded jackets and sealskin boots. Their hair was thick, straight and dark; they had yellow almond-shaped eyes and strong white teeth (not that any of them smiled). They were fierce and unfriendly, and did indeed have bows and arrows as the boy had said.

The air swished and an arrow landed at Ollimun's feet.

'Speak quickly,' commanded the boy.

Ollimun took half a step forward. 'I give you my word as a wizard that my companions and I mean you no harm. We are no friends of the goblins. Far from it. All we ask is a safe passage through your lands and we will be gone.'

Wizard. The word raced excitedly around the ring of snowmen.

'Are you the kind of wizard who heals the sick?'

'That is *one* of my qualities,' said Ollimun modestly.

Agna touched Temmi's shoulder. 'The ring of snowmen is widening! I believe they're moving away.'

It was true—although Temmi never caught a movement, the snowmen seemed to retreat bit by bit (some might even say *melt away* but for the fact this gave the wrong impression). Slowly they disappeared into the forest, leaving behind a raggle-taggle band of children, some with babies strapped to their backs. Looking at them, Temmi decided the rule must be, anyone old enough to hold something, carried a weapon. Those without bows and arrows had spears or harpoons; and those who were really small and could manage nothing bigger were a danger only to themselves with knives made out of walrus bone.

'Where are your parents?' asked Ollimun, searching amongst them for an older face.

The boy who had done most of the talking shrugged. 'Away,' he said. 'There have been reports of goblins on the edge of our land. Our parents have gone to see if they are true. If they are, they will fight them.'

'The reports are indeed true, we crossed them ourselves not a day ago.' The wizard half closed his eyes and considered matters. 'I understand now about the enchanted snowmen,' he said. 'They must be your guardians while your parents are away.'

'*We* can take care of ourselves,' said the boy proudly.

Waving at the others to put away their weapons and repair the damaged snowmen that had been left behind, he strode forward, pulled the shot arrow from the snow and replaced it in the willow-bark quiver on his back.

'My name is Soy,' he said. 'We are the Eckmo people. And if you are as good a wizard as your beard is long, you have arrived just in time to help my older brother, Mau.'

'Why, what is wrong with him?' asked Temmi. He saw by Soy's face that he was trying to hide his concern with a show of fierceness.

'Oh, you know how pig-headed big brothers can be,' he said. 'Mine went hunting in the forest alone—even though our father had forbidden it. A wolf came. The snowmen guardians were not quick enough to stop it, and the wolf—a giant of a creature to judge by its paw-prints—sprang at Mau and tore into him with a savage bite.'

'Sounds very much like Frostbite's doing,' Temmi whispered to Agna. She nodded.

'Then take me to your brother at once,' said Ollimun.

Away, waiting in the trees, were a number of sledges joined to teams of large white foxes. Temmi was as surprised to see the beautiful sleek creatures as Soy must have been to see a flying bear, but this was not the time to stand and wonder at them. Everyone found a place on board a sledge; Agna pulled up a fur to keep her legs warm, and Soy took up the driver's position at the back of the biggest sledge. Before him eight pairs of foxes rose obediently.

'Yah!' He cracked the whip. 'Away, Ghost! Fly, Blizzard!'

The foxes bounded forward with eager barks and tiny bells jangling on their harnesses. In a matter of seconds they found their pace, moving swiftly and easily across the snow. Trees flew past and the cold air stung the riders' faces; it even frosted Temmi's eyebrows. Glancing up from time to time he saw Cush flying alongside, but always at a distance from the foxes.

After several miles of travelling like this, the

forest suddenly fell back around a snowy clearing where, as evening fell, silent groups of snowmen guardians were gathering to keep watch among the fringes of the trees. This was because in the centre of the clearing stood a village built entirely of ice, every house a perfect dome clustering around a much larger dome. Temmi guessed the larger building was a meeting place for Soy's people, rather like the longhouse in his own village. This turned out to be the case.

The village had no streets or lanes, instead narrow passageways were cut through the snow. Leaving Cush outside, Soy led the way by lantern to the great ice dome. Temmi was surprised to find it not at all cold. He undid his cloak and saw it was even possible to have a fire here without melting the walls. The fire was large and welcoming, and the smoke rose in a column and left through a round hole in the roof. Soot speckled the roof like black stars.

Next to the fire lay Mau, a thin, pale boy draped in furs. The few youngsters who had been left behind to take care of him stepped aside without a word, glad to let the wizard take their place.

'Hmm.'

Ollimun peeled back the furs and examined him.

'The child has a fever and his arm is more badly ripped than I imagined,' he said, casually throwing some scented herbs on to the fire.

'Will he die?' demanded Soy.

'He will if the poison in his arm spreads to the rest of him. Now do exactly as I say—'

Ollimun snapped out his orders, sending for clean towels and jugs of fresh water, honey and bandages, and strong tea for himself. Magic then followed, magic of the best and most wholesome sort.

And, as is the case when magic is good, it became a performance—something to watch, with plenty of breathtaking moments along the way.

Sitting on the stepped ice seats at the base of the wall, the tribe of children hung on to the wizard's every word and movement. Soy was still and tense, his eyes staring like a hawk's and his shoulders heavy beneath the arms of friends. Younger children drooped with tiredness, yet still clutched their bone knives in their tight little fists. Now and again a baby cried and had to be nursed back to sleep. And sometimes, for their own comfort, the children began to hum: one long note, with voices joining and falling away until it dwindled back into silence, broken only by Ollimun demanding a root be cut up. 'And not too fine!'

His magic took many forms. Wand magic, touch magic, wish magic, word magic. The end result a sweet-smelling potion bubbling over the fire. Then, setting it aside to cool, he saw to the bandaging of Mau's arm, carefully slipping in a different leaf at each turn, and finally tying the bandage with a special knot to prevent ugly scars from forming. Then back to the potion—which he tested with a finger; and using his finger again, he dripped a little into Mau's mouth at a time until the right amount was given.

'There, it is done,' he said, wearily straightening his back. 'The poison's spread has been stopped and this potion will act quickly to make him well and strong. Give it to him twice a day with a wooden spoon—but not oak.'

Confident of what would happen next, the wizard quietly set about clearing away the clutter he had made, stacking the dirty bowls and gathering up the used herbs. He didn't turn around or look the least bit surprised when Mau's eyes flickered open and he asked in a puzzled voice where the great wolf had gone.

Soy was overjoyed. 'Wizard, thank you. *Thank you*. If there's any favour I can do in return, just tell me and it will be done.'

Ollimun allowed himself a sly smile—why, he

already had the very thing in mind . . . Later he found Agna and Temmi sitting close by the fire, warming their stockinged toes.

'Our good deed is rewarded!' he announced. 'I've told Soy our story and he has agreed to be our guide and take us by sledge to Grimskalk's mountain.'

'Can he get us there in time for the next full moon?' asked Agna.

Ollimun's eyes gleamed. 'The dear boy assures me he can!'

Chapter Twelve

Stars still shone in a black sky when Soy awoke them early the following morning; later the frost-hardened snow would crunch under their boots. Soy made his way down a passage to the fox house. From the sleeping huddles of fur he pulled out his best runners. He took his time and chose carefully, he wanted to be sure he had the fastest team.

When Temmi stepped outdoors ten minutes later, the sledge stood ready. The foxes shook their heads. The harness bells tinkled. It sounded as if the cold had found a voice. Ollimun and Agna came out. Like Temmi, Agna had borrowed a fur-trimmed coat, which was much warmer than any of her own clothes. She stamped her feet and slapped her sides; her yawn smoked in the cold.

'Can you see Cush?' she asked.

Temmi peered into the surrounding trees until he spotted him, nestled amongst the branches. He could tell at once the bear was sulking. Not because he had been left outside—Cush was a wild bear, after all—but because he felt ignored and jealous of the foxes.

'Don't worry, he'll be friendly enough when we stop for breakfast,' Temmi told her.

Nearby he noticed a group of children, who out of curiosity had come to watch them leave. Their hoods were up and their noses ran in the bitter cold; one or two chewed strips of dried reindeer meat. They had set their lanterns on the ground.

'You really going to Grimskalk's mountain?' demanded a small sleepy girl with the grubbiest face imaginable. 'Aren't you scared she'll eat you?'

'Dragons only like little girls,' said Soy earnestly as he tightened straps about the sledge. And to an older girl next to her he said, 'Ollah, take good care of my brother for me. If Mau refuses to take his medicine, pinch his nose until he does.'

'Don't worry, I'll be harder on him than his own mother,' promised Ollah. 'I've already had to order him back to bed. He was looking for his coat and boots so he could come with you.'

'In that case we'll leave quickly so he can't try again . . . Everyone aboard!'

Soy himself was last to take up his place. 'I'll be back as soon as I can,' he called.

These words were also his farewell, for with a crack of the whip he drove the foxes forward, the sledge sliding smoothly behind. And from the corner of his eye Temmi watched as Cush stretched his wings and grumpily followed.

Together they sped through the forest, the only sounds to be heard at that hour the swish of the sledge's metal runners and the panting of the foxes. But if they thought themselves alone, a careful look into the trees was bound to reveal one of the ever-watchful guardians, growing fewer in number the further they went away from the Eckmo's lands.

For four days they travelled by sledge, making excellent progress and covering many more miles than was possible on foot. Camped up on the fourth night, Ollimun took out his skin-maps and was delighted to find he now needed only one to show their position. It was the map with the tiny dragon on top of a mountain.

He chuckled contentedly. 'If all goes well,

tomorrow we reach our destination. And tomorrow is the night of the full moon when Grimskalk must leave her mountain and go in search of treasure.'

Hearing this, Temmi had mixed feelings—he wondered what dangers might lie ahead.

Dawn came late the following morning. Low thick cloud deadened the light. Against it Cush shone as brightly as a snowflake as he swooped after the sledge. The weather was changing. Dark clouds hid the tops of distant mountains, while each new breath of wind carried a scattering of snow.

'There's going to be a storm,' called Soy, but this was news to no one.

The blizzard finally broke some time in the early afternoon. It met them head on—a fully made tempest—howling in all its fury. Cush, caught out by it high up in open sky, crashed to earth like a tangled kite, crying to be rescued. 'Come on, boy,' said Temmi as he and Ollimun dragged him aboard the sledge, Cush bad-temperedly chewing off his broken feathers. The snow quickly thickened. Squinting up his eyes, Temmi found he could no longer make out the line of foxes in front of him. Lanterns might have helped, but the gale blew them out as quickly as they were lit (and lighting them was no easy matter in the first place). The sledge went slower and slower, and the foxes bowed their heads into the storm and suffered dreadfully.

'It's no use,' hollered Soy above the roaring wind. 'We'll soon be at a standstill. We'll have to give up the sledge!'

'We must do whatever must be done,' came back Ollimun's reply.

Soy said he knew of some caves up ahead where the foxes could be safely holed-up until their return. It took forever to reach them, the foxes close to exhaustion; and although time was scarce, Soy made sure his animals had a good dry cave that faced out of the wind, with enough food and water to last several days. Cush, however, could not be persuaded to join them.

Agna checked in her pocket to see that Icicle was safe, then turned slowly to the mouth of the cave. The snow seemed to be falling in horizontal lines, churning around the entrance like smoke.

'I suppose we must go back out into it,' she said wearily.

'Here,' said Ollimun, 'put this inside your glove.' He gave each of them a small glowing ball, which immediately made them feel warmer.

'It was something I was saving,' said Ollimun.

The enchantment was a small but welcome comfort. The only one to be had. Outside, the storm fell upon them like a starving animal, the air seemed to have claws; and the snow was now so deep that every few steps Cush had to be pulled free by his scruff.

Step by step Soy led the way. He was their guide. As the snow raced in a thickening blur and the trees turned to smudges of darkness, they followed him without a word.

Temmi had given up the idea of asking him how much further it was. He stumbled to his knees. His eyes ached, his face stung, and as Ollimun's spell wore thin, the cold came biting through his clothes. In front of him he saw the wizard pulling himself along by his wand, his beard weighed down with ice like dribbles of hard candle wax.

For a long while nobody noticed Soy acting strangely—turning his head this way and that in an ever more desperate manner. (It was hard to notice anything beyond the blue tips of their own noses.) But in the end, after much stopping and starting and sudden changes in direction, nobody could be in the slightest doubt that he was lost, and they were lost with him.

The storm became its most frenzied then.

'What are we going to do?' cried Agna.

Soy looked confused. He blinked away fat snowflakes from his lashes—and others immediately stuck there. 'I-I'll try calling on the snow guardians for help. But I don't know if their magic is strong enough to reach us here . . . We're so far from my village, you see . . .'

'Call them,' said Ollimun calmly. 'Good magic will see out the distance however great.'

Soy closed his eyes and concentrated. His call was silent like a prayer. Temmi rubbed his hands and stamped his feet, waiting, the grey wind coiling around him.

'There! I see something—' Suddenly Agna was shouting excitedly. She ploughed forward before Temmi saw what it was.

When he and the others caught up with her, she was standing beside a snowman. He was hardly more than a half tumbled heap of snow, yet his arm, made from a single twig, pointed like a signpost. They went that way gladly and fifty paces later reached a second, similar snowman; it led to another and that to another and that to another, like links in a chain. But the snowmen were poor broken things and Agna nearly wept frozen tears just to see them: especially as they crumbled into nothing once their job was done.

Slowly a large grey shape loomed in the distance.

Soy was overjoyed. 'That's *it*—we're there!' he cried. 'That's Castle Surewall. It was abandoned centuries ago when Grimskalk took over the mountain next to it. On a clear day you can see the dragon as plainly as you can see me.'

'On a clear day,' huffed Ollimun unimpressed.

Approaching the castle on its sheltered side, they discovered surprisingly little snow on the broad steps leading up to it. The steps were cut into living rock and rose twisting and turning to a shattered gatehouse. They entered, clambering over broken stones, a crumbling arch soaring over them. They felt so relieved. They were out of the storm at last.

Beyond the gatehouse lay a great many ruined buildings, all with empty rooms inside; the ceilingless ones filled up to their doorheads in snow. Yet it didn't take long to find a tiny guardroom that was dry and sheltered enough to set up camp. For firewood they needed to look no further than the rotten rafters lying about them. And once Ollimun had used his wand to spark them alight, flames sprang up as bright as spring flowers, immediately lifting their spirits before their outstretched hands could benefit from any real warmth. Supper was less inspiring: dried rations from their bundles, even for Cush; and melted snow to drink.

Tired, fed, and feeling relatively contented, the company dozed by the fire while the storm raged on outside. For several long hours it hurled tiles and slammed shutters like an angry spoilt child . . . And then, with a few last blusters, it stopped. Like a candle it had blown itself out and the suddenness of it doing so made Ollimun lift his nodding head. Temmi shook his ears, unused to the silence.

For Ollimun the ending of the storm was the very thing he had been waiting for. He slowly got to his feet.

'Where are you going?' asked Temmi watching him.

Ollimun shushed him. The others were soundly asleep; Cush's wings twitching as he dreamed.

'No need to wake them. Not yet,' said the wizard. 'Come, Temmi, you and I will go and see if the full moon is up.'

They went out across a small snowy courtyard with a well at its centre. Temmi noticed how cold it was—then he noticed the stars. At the edge of the sky the last wisps of storm clouds raced from view, leaving behind stars so big and bright that he stopped and stared up at them, trembling at their severe beauty.

'Come on, boy,' he heard Ollimun mutter gruffly. 'It's not the stars we want but the moon.'

They went on until they reached one of the castle's many watchtowers. Its tight twisting stairway rose windowless. In the darkness Temmi heard Ollimun grunt for breath, heard his wand tap-tapping against stone; and then they reached the top and stepped out.

High up, the air was so crisp that each breath froze Temmi inside; looking down he saw his hands were blue—not from cold, but blue with starlight.

'There, what a sight,' breathed Ollimun, staring at the moon rising between two distant mountains. Gradually, as the moon rose, the snow turned from palest blue to palest gold, and everything appeared in clearest detail—and one thing in particular.

All at once Temmi was scrabbling to get away. Had Ollimun not reached out and grabbed him, he would have fallen back right to the bottom of the stairs. He held Temmi close to him in the folds of his cloak until he was calm.

'Is that her?' whispered Temmi wide eyed.

'If you mean is that our dragon, then yes—yes, it is. That is Grimskalk, and that is her mountain, and that is where what we have come to do begins and ends.'

'But . . . *she's gigantic.*'

'She wouldn't be a proper dragon if she didn't make you tremble at the knees.'

Smooth and glistening, Grimskalk coiled herself tightly around her mountain. Three times her body went around it. Her claws pressed their points deep into the rock; and with each of her breaths she gave birth to a new cloud—a real cloud that let fall a scattering of snowflakes.

As Temmi watched, a moonbeam crept up her scaly back and reached her great head. Grimskalk opened one eye. It was as if a powerful beam of green light had turned on. Twin beams when her other eye opened; and together they scoured the land like searchlights.

Temmi once more took fright. Pulling on the wizard's sleeve he cried, 'Come away, Ollimun, before she sees us!'

But nothing would make Ollimun move. He stood proudly before the dragon's glare, his face and cloak bathed in green.

'Don't fret, boy. Her mind is on treasure, not on a little, tasteless, boy-shaped snack like you. She knows she must leave soon and begin her search.'

For Temmi, her leaving couldn't come quick enough—the dragon terrified him.

'This is the moment now,' said the wizard in a voice both flat and thrilling.

Temmi forced himself to take notice. The she-dragon had begun to stir, had begun to uncoil herself from around the mountain, avalanches of snow sliding off her sides. Her head towered over the mountain top and her eyes beamed out into the black universe. Then from deep inside her a growl started its journey upwards, beginning as a rumble in her stomach and working its way through her body like an explosion in a mine. Her jaws parted revealing a rock forest of twisted fangs and out burst a sound made of many other sounds, and like all the storm's rage pressed into a single moment. The castle shook and walls cracked and plaster came crashing down.

As if winded, Temmi took a moment to recover. When next he looked he saw the land shadowed by the dragon's outstretched wings. They fanned for lift, bending tree tops, snapping branches, and stirring up the snow into short-lived whirlwinds . . . yet slowly, very slowly, she rose, gathering strength and blotting out ten thousand stars. With height she was able to fly freely. Twice she circled the mountain—twice her eyes swept over the land, then with a thunder-crack whip of her tail, she plunged northwards and was gone.

Ollimun and Temmi watched her go, and although it is impossible to believe, she soon shrank to the size of a dot and even *that* vanished a second later.

'Good hunting to her,' wished Ollimun, turning away towards the stairs. 'And good hunting to us too. Hurry, Temmi, it is time to wake the others.'

Chapter Thirteen

Yawning and unhappy at having to leave their warm, comfortable fireside, the others followed Temmi and Ollimun out of the castle into deep uneven snow—the dragon's mountain rising directly ahead: a single peak giving no clue as to why it was so special. Agna stumbled, barely half awake; and Cush couldn't understand what was so important that it couldn't be done in the morning. He flew ahead and sat waiting impatiently in the snow.

Although Temmi's bones ached with weariness, his head was remarkably clear. Turning back he viewed Castle Surewall properly for the very first time. Ruined as it was, it remained an impressive sight with over twenty crumbling, snow-capped towers along its length. Other buildings clustered together, the rafters of the great hall resembling ribs sticking out of the snow. Along the outer walls were long scratch marks. Between yawns Soy told him this was where Grimskalk sharpened her claws.

No wonder men had quickly abandoned the place, thought Temmi.

In silence they crossed snow and moonlight, a trailing shadow at each pair of heels. Before them a soft breeze brushed away loose crumbs of snow, making a faint scratching sound, but more often there was a deep stillness.

Cush returned. He flew back quickly, the smell of dragon making him uneasy and in need of his friends. Watching the bear come swooping lightly down, Temmi suddenly envied him: he longed to have wings of his own and know what it is to be lighter than air—*to fly like an angel* . . . But instead he had to make do with feet and big clumsy boots; and the only way for him to reach the dragon's mountain was down a narrow gorge littered with loose icy pebbles. They made walking difficult. Each of the company took a turn to slip on them. Agna woke up completely after taking *her* jolt. Running north–south, the gorge squeezed the gentle breeze into a chill wind, blowing sharp snow crystals off the rocky ledges into their eyes.

And as the wind stiffened and the shadows deepened, Grimskalk's mountain seemed to grow higher and higher before them. Its sides were black rock streaked with knobbly ice and deeply marked by the dragon's clinging claws. A large hole near the top was the only opening that Temmi could see. He supposed it was through this that Grimskalk dropped her treasure when she returned home after a successful hunt. For dragons (and angels and flying bears for that matter) it was an easy doorway; for Temmi and his friends in their big clumsy boots, however, it was impossible.

'How *are* we to get inside the mountain?' Agna asked Ollimun, thinking the same thoughts as Temmi.

Ollimun pretended not to hear; he pretended he was having trouble on the icy pebbles. He did everything, in fact, except answer her question.

And suddenly Temmi understood why. 'You don't know *how* to get into the mountain, do you?' he cried. 'How could you, wizard? To bring us all this way for nothing! To have us fail at the very last moment! And when the dragon flies back I expect she'll find us frozen like statues on her doorstep, *still trying to find the way in——*'

'Enough, boy!'

Now it was Ollimun's turn to be angry. He banged down his wand.

'Haven't you learnt anything about magic by now? Haven't you learnt to trust it? There are bound to be many entrances into the mountain. Secret entrances. Have faith and keep watching.'

'What do we watch for?' asked Soy, but Ollimun was too busy mumbling to himself and did not reply.

Perhaps the wizard's magic was already at work, for they had not gone more than a dozen steps when Soy spotted something glittering on the ground. It glittered differently to snow and frost, and as soon as it caught his eye he bent down and picked it up.

'A golden coin,' he said in surprise. 'And over there, there are others.'

'Spills from Grimskalk's treasure,' explained Ollimun. 'Dragons carry their treasure tightly clenched in their jaws. Awkward, but their only way. Sometimes accidents occur. I've even heard cases of it raining gold.'

Soy went to put the coin into his pocket and was stopped only by the frown on Ollimun's face.

'Throw it away, boy. Remember that dragons' treasure is cursed.'

Soy gave the coin a last wistful look then flipped it aside.

A hand, rather like a hairless paw and as small and neat as a child's, came darting out from behind a rock and snatched the coin up. Before anyone could be surprised by this, the creature showed itself completely. It dashed out, busily picking up the other coins that lay nearby and slipping them into a satchel.

At first Temmi thought it was a peculiar child, but that was mainly because of its size. Then he noticed that the creature had wisps of fine colourless hair and a skin so pale that Temmi could practically see through to its bones. It was drably dressed and barefoot and wore spectacles of thick dark glass—showing how sensitive it was to light, even softest moonlight.

Not caring about the small band who now followed its every movement, the creature stopped at an old dead tree, staring up at several fabulous necklaces dangling in its branches. Without hesitation the creature climbed up and soon the jewels were retrieved, the creature tucking them safely away along with the coins.

'What a strange little thing,' said Agna. 'What is it called?'

'A grubling,' replied Ollimun. 'Where you have

dragons you are bound to find grublings. The two live side by side, mainly because grublings love treasure as much as dragons do. And although they never have treasure of their own, dragons have learned to put up with them because they make such useful little caretakers. Watch it carefully.' He shot Temmi a look. 'If we follow it, it may show us a way inside.'

Hurrying, sometimes leaping from boulder to boulder but never once glancing back or stopping to rest its heavy satchel, the grubling led them further down the gorge. And if it did pause briefly, it was certain to pluck a jewel or coin from the snow. And treasure was not the only thing to be found lying there. At the foot of the mountain were the remains of Grimskalk's past dinners: whale bones and elephants' jaws and mammoths' tusks—picked clean and flung aside.

Suddenly Ollimun stopped dead, holding up his hand to halt the others. They saw that the grubling had come to a halt too.

'Ah, this looks promising.'

'What's that strange music?' asked Agna.

'The grubling—it's talking to the mountain.'

'*Talking*? It sounds more like birdsong or a penny whistle.'

This was true. By no means was it a commanding voice, yet the mountain obeyed it at once. It opened with a deep rumble, and closed again once the grubling was safely inside.

'Come on,' said Ollimun.

They hurried forward and took up the grubling's place without seeing any sign of the entrance.

'We have the door, now all we need is a door handle,' said the wizard, and saying this he drove his wand deep into the rock with all his might. Sparks flew as it pierced the mountainside. Of course the wand hadn't really become a handle (that was far too neat), it was more like a lever. If they wanted to get inside the mountain they had first the job of forcing open the door. Gripping his wand in both hands, Ollimun pushed as hard as he could. After several minutes the mountain opened with a creak—but only as wide as his finger.

Ollimun threw his beard over his shoulder, sweating despite the cold. 'Well? Are you going to stand watching or are you going to help?' he demanded.

Temmi, Soy, and Agna rushed up to lend a hand, Temmi amazed that the wand did not break; yet in the end it proved stronger than rock.

Bit by bit they forced open the door.

'We did it,' said Soy springing aside to admire their work.

'Yes,' said Ollimun straightening his beard, 'and we had better leave it open in case we have need of a swift escape.' He glanced at the moon as if it were his own pocket-watch showing how much time they had left.

They went inside—Ollimun, Temmi, Agna, Soy, and Cush—all standing closely together in a pool of wand-light. Beyond it there was very little to see, just a long, straight passageway sloping gently upwards. Mercifully, it did not smell or drip with slime the way goblin holes did. And there in the distance they saw their grubling hurrying on. They had no idea where it was going, but it made sense to follow it all the same.

They set off, on the way meeting no traps or fortified gates or fierce growling animals standing guard. For why would they be needed? Ollimun told them that the curse was enough to put off most thieves. Anyone who did try to steal from a dragon was either very, very clever or very, very stupid.

'Look,' said Soy. 'The passageway's coming to an end.'

'Ah, the heart of the mountain.'

'And look, Ollimun,' said Agna. 'Icicle knows it's nearly home . . . and I think it's glad.'

She pulled it from her pocket and everyone was forced to turn away, dazzled by the needle-sharp rays of light that streamed from its centre. Carefully Agna wrapped it in her handkerchief and Temmi stopped seeing stars.

Going on a few more paces, they learnt the secret of Grimskalk's mountain. It was *hollow*—the hole through which Grimskalk dropped her treasure appearing high above their heads. And they saw that some way below the opening, the walls were carved into galleries, leading to other passageways and caves; and along these galleries hundreds of grublings moved in a steady silent flow, not one bothering to give the company a second glance.

'It reminds me of a hive,' said Temmi, whose grandfather used to keep bees. 'Everyone is so busy.'

'Didn't I tell you they were useful little caretakers,' said Ollimun. 'All we need to do now is find the treasure caves and return Icicle to its rightful place.'

The caves on the first level appeared to be for general storage and supplies. Those on the second level were long plain dormitories where the day-

shift workers slept. On the third level there were workshops, rows of grublings repairing and polishing, working by the light of a few faintly glowing crystals. But nowhere did the company come across anything that might be described as a treasure cave.

'We'll keep going on till we find them,' said Ollimun.

Grublings swarmed about them along the galleries, carrying chests and a host of precious objects. They winced a little at the wizard's pale wand-light, but didn't try to stop anyone from going wherever they pleased. Indeed, Temmi found the most troublesome thing about grublings was endlessly having to push his way through them—it was as much a chore as trying to swim upstream.

Then finally they arrived at the fourth level, and the first cave on it gleamed promisingly. Temmi peered a little closer into the gloom.

'It's full of thrones,' he said with a gasp of disbelief.

It was true and made a startling sight—even for Agna who had lived most of her life in a palace. Empty thrones made of gold, silver, jade, and ivory were lined in rows stretching away into the shadows, each throne more fabulous than the one next to it. And to keep them from tarnishing and to stop the spiders from setting up their webs, groups of grublings silently worked away, polishing the thrones' many arms and legs and great tall backs carved with shields and lions. They totally ignored the company—even Cush when he decided to leap up on one of the silk tasselled cushions. Showing no surprise or anger, the grublings simply polished around him as if he wasn't there.

'Go ahead, Agna,' said Ollimun quietly, standing aside for her.

Agna took out Icicle. She unwrapped it from her handkerchief and found it no longer shone. Holding it gently in her hand she stepped into the cave. 'Go on,' said the wizard behind her. Agna nodded. But as she started to put it down, the grublings stopped work and noisily crowded around her. She was frightened. Their piping voices sounded like an angry dawn chorus. They blocked Agna's way and slowly, without roughness, drove her out of the cave.

'I don't understand,' she cried. 'Don't they want Icicle?'

Ollimun didn't understand either. 'Come on, we'll try the next cave.'

This they smelt before they reached. It smelt of

salt and seaweed and rotten wood, hardly surprising when they saw the great ship-wrecked galleon housed there, its sails in tatters and rigging hanging down. At that moment it was crewed by grublings who lined every deck, brushing and shovelling off showers of golden doubloons, while heaps more coins spilt out of a long gash in the ship's side (along with the whitened bones of several unfortunate pirates).

'Grimskalk must have dived to the bottom of an ocean to claim that prize,' said Ollimun.

Plundered doubloons stretched around the ship in drifts while a second gang of grublings waded through them, turning loose coins into neat counted piles. Here and there larger objects stuck out like driftwood floating in a golden sea. Crowns, dishes, silver helmets, and goblets—most encrusted with barnacles and trailing strings of dried seaweed.

'Try again,' Ollimun told Agna.

She did and with the same result: before she could leave Icicle, a mob of grublings noisily drove her away. Nor was it any different in the third cave they visited, a cave of precious gems, glinting in the light of Ollimun's wand like the eyes of a snow leopard—some stones as cold as frost, others flickering as if about to burst into flames.

'Time's running out,' said Agna worriedly. 'If I don't hand Icicle over soon, the curse will not be lifted.'

'There must be a reason why.' Ollimun thought hard, drumming his fingers on his wand. 'Silver—gold—gemstones,' he kept muttering. Then he gave a shout. 'Of course! Icicle is far more precious than any of those. There must be another cave somewhere—a place for Grimskalk's extra special treasures. And we have to find exactly where it is.'

As he said this there arose a commotion below. The grublings who polished the gemstones didn't turn a hair at it. But when Temmi and the others rushed out and peered over the gallery, they were dismayed.

'Tin Nose!' said Temmi.

'And Frostbite with him,' said Agna.

'And,' said Ollimun bleakly, 'enough goblins to do a hundred years' worth of mischief.'

Chapter Fourteen

'But how did they know we were here?' said Agna.

'Tracks are easy to follow in snow,' murmured Ollimun gloomily.

He was right—but this told only half the tale. Having survived the underground landslide, Tin Nose had driven his goblins hard across snow and through mountains, the goblins sometimes riding the backs of wolves for speed; Frostbite and the remainder of the pack pulling Tin Nose on his sledge.

Twice they had nearly lost the company's trail. The first time was in that strange forest where snowmen had appeared, blocking their way. Tin

Nose had ordered his men to go around them, picking up the tracks of a sledge on the other side. Then there was the great blizzard that came from nowhere and made the world like new, levelling old drifts and heaping up new ones that were twice as high. Yet by this time Tin Nose had guessed where the company was headed: there was nowhere else to make for but the dragon's mountain.

And all the while, Tin Nose's mind was so full of rage and bitterness towards Temmi and the other escaped prisoners, thinking up new ways to make them suffer when he caught them, that he quite failed to notice how rebellious his own men were getting. They were cold and miserable and far away from their beloved holes; and Stagdog was able to move amongst them, whispering, plotting and stirring.

Now, they were all here in the dragon's mountain and things were starting to happen. The grublings, Temmi noticed, had silently disappeared from the galleries; not so much to escape the goblins as the light from their fiery torches. But more importantly things were also happening amongst the goblins themselves.

'We had better go on with the search,' said Temmi stepping away, but Ollimun pulled him back.

'There is something brewing down there,' he said. 'Something poisonous. It may repay a moment's delay to find out what.'

High up, they had a good clear view. The goblins, they saw, stood in a dense ring around Tin Nose and Frostbite. Tin Nose looked a fearful sight. His false nose bristled with spikes, as did the shoulders of his armour. On his breastplate was a wolf's head, jaws parted as if about to attack; smaller wolves at the top of each arm. He moved restlessly. Stiff legged, he strode up and down in his clanking metal suit, his helmet under his arm.

'Did you not hear me?' he roared. 'I gave you an order—see it done at once!'

Not a goblin moved, only the flames of their torches stirred.

'*Well!*'

Stagdog stepped forward, his scraps of armour unpolished and dirty. He drew his sword—his faithful cutter—and for a moment Temmi thought he was going to use it against Tin Nose. Frostbite, thinking the same, growled a soft, menacing warning.

Then Stagdog spoke, his voice a joyful hiss.

'The goblins are not your slaves, Tin Nose. You are not our ma-ster. You are not even our friend. Your words are empty wind-blasts. Go order yourself, little human.'

'*Stagdog*, how dare you speak in such a tone and stand looking at me with that brazen gleam in your eye. You have gone too far this time—this is treason. I shall have you put into a barrel of stones and thrown off a cliff. Fros—'

Before he could call up his wolf, Stagdog cried, 'Nets!' And the goblins, who must have been waiting for Stagdog's word, cast their nets, so that in seconds Tin Nose and Frostbite were helplessly tangled up in them. Then many eager hands rushed to help pull the pair off their feet; Tin Nose's armour clattering as he struck the ground.

An approving roar went up at this, followed by the chant, 'Stagdog—Stagdog—Stagdog . . . '

Stagdog leapt upon Tin Nose's chest and appeared to them waving his cutter triumphantly in the air.

'What about the treasure you promised us, Stagdog?' shouted a voice.

'Treasure!' screamed Stagdog excitedly. 'You want treasure?' He kept stamping and grinding his heel on Tin Nose's breastplate. 'Look around you, brothers. These are treasure halls. Go help yourselves deep, I say. Take as much clutch as you can stagger under.'

'But what about the dragon's curse?'

Stagdog danced carelessly on top of his enemy. 'You think a curse can reach us goblins once we are safe underground? Why waste these moments, brothers, when you could be doing what us goblins do best—*thieving*. Follow me—I lead the way!'

'*Raaah!*'

Needing no further encouragement, the goblins stormed the caves and galleries. From the first, there was much pushing and elbowing; squabbles quickly turning into noisy fights. The drummers— all of one greedy mind—ripped the top skins off their drums ready to fill them like jewellery boxes. In a matter of seconds Tin Nose and Frostbite were left struggling in their nets alone; and Temmi remembered Ollimun's words—to steal from a dragon you had to be either very, very clever—or very, very stupid . . .

Ollimun had seen enough. 'Now we must use our time well. The mountain will be overrun by goblins before we know it.'

There were many more treasure caves left to explore but these turned out to be very much like the first three. Oh, they contained treasure, of every dazzling kind—but none of it special in the way Icicle was; and everything was simply heaped up or spilling out of splitting chests. Temmi groaned, he was sick of the sight of gold; his feelings for it the exact opposite to the goblins', who were hot and excited—if not driven mad— with gold fever. And at each new cave they came to, the grublings were sure to come crowding around, driving Agna and Icicle away.

'Wand—help us!' commanded Ollimun, the sound of goblin howls growing closer by the second.

The wand began to glow orange and drag the wizard's arm. It pointed to a cave on the next level.

'*That must be it! That must be the one!*' cried Ollimun. 'We are nearly there.'

Agna clutched Icicle ready in her hand as Temmi and Soy each grabbed one of the wizard's sleeves, pulling him along; Cush keeping pace in the air.

The cave was the last in the mountain. Temmi knew at once it was the one they wanted when he saw it was full of all things magical, and the walls lined with books. Ollimun called it a *library*, a word Temmi had never heard before.

'Lie-bury.' He said it to himself. He supposed it was a *lie-bury* because many ancient, crumbling books were *lying* around, while grubling scholars had their heads *buried* inside them.

Each scholar worked at a stone table lit by a few yellow crystals, not only reading but learning a book by heart, and by doing so—by storing the knowledge inside him—turning himself into the dragon's *living* treasure. The scholars were busy and did not look up from their tasks, nor did they come crowding around Agna, insisting she go away.

'Look,' said Soy. 'One is coming up. He's carrying a glass box. It's for you, Agna, he wants you to put Icicle inside.'

'Well, he can't have it—not just yet. He'll just have to wait!'

They all stared at her. Agna blinked and seemed a little surprised herself.

'I mean,' she went on less sharply, 'I only want to hold it a moment longer. There's no harm in it, not just for a moment.'

'Agna,' said Ollimun firmly, 'it is always hard giving up something magical, but listen to me. You *must* hand it back. You must break the curse. Do it now while you have the chance.'

'I . . . It's . . . ' Agna shut her eyes, holding out Icicle with a shaky hand. 'There,' she said, laying it gently in the box.

And they heard a crack as the curse broke.

Temmi grinned and hugged her. But that was

as long (or as short) as their happiness lasted. Long fingers suddenly shot forward and snatched Icicle from where it lay.

'What is this? Magic? I know it is magic, I can smell magic.'

Temmi turned sharply and saw Stagdog. The ridiculous creature resembled a Christmas tree. Gold chains and pearl necklaces were looped around his neck. Every finger and toe gleamed with rings; diamonds shone in his pointed ears, and his pockets bulged, spilling jewels as carelessly as crumbs. But he was not to be laughed at, not while his cutter was drawn and waved in the air.

'Put it back, goblin,' said Ollimun bluntly. 'There is plenty of treasure in this mountain if it's loot you want.'

'Holdtongue, wizard,' squawked Stagdog. 'You think I don't know what this is? You think that Stagdog doesn't know it is the she-dragon's lodestone, the greatest treasure of all?' He grinned crookedly. 'With one call on this the dragon is duty-bound to come and serve me *and only me— Stagdog the goblin. Stagdog the Great!*'

'No!' roared Ollimun reaching out to snatch the lodestone back. But Stagdog was quicker. His cheeks filled and he blew a short sharp blast.

Temmi and Agna covered their ears against the

awful noise. The mountain trembled, loose stones rattled down, and heavy books toppled over or came crashing down off the shelves.

And the mountain was not the only thing that trembled, for Icicle had one last test for those who wished to be master over Grimskalk. It made the brave feel braver, and the strong realize their strength; while those who were like Stagdog, suddenly saw what weak and cowardly dogs they were.

Horrified at the power he had unleashed, Stagdog let Icicle drop from his grasp, rubbing his lips hard where they had touched it, and slowly and nervously backing away. He tried to speak but, overwhelmed by a creeping terror, he turned on his big flat feet and fled, joining the ranks of howling goblins who streamed from the mountain, dropping treasure as they went.

Within minutes peace returned. At their tables, each grubling scholar simply dusted the page before him and continued to read. Icicle lay on the ground where Stagdog had dropped it. Picking it up, Ollimun polished it on his beard and carefully replaced it in its box.

'Take it away and make sure no one but the dragon knows where it is hidden.'

The grubling bowed and left.

'Now we must leave too,' said Ollimun briskly. 'The call has been made and wherever she is, Grimskalk will have heard it. She will forget all thoughts of treasure and fly straight back. Stagdog was right about that.'

'Good,' said Soy. 'She'll catch the goblins red-handed stealing her treasure.'

'Which is no more than they deserve,' said Agna. 'Although you can't help feeling a little bit sorry for them too.'

'Humph,' said Soy.

They set off, and as they hurried down the galleries, the grublings slowly came out of hiding. They didn't give Temmi and his friends a second glance; however, this is not to say they passed unnoticed by everyone . . .

'Here—over here. Release us at once!' bellowed a voice from the tangle of nets.

'My, my, Tin Nose,' tutted Agna. 'Where are your manners? Away with the goblins?'

'Those green-skinned traitors!'

Tin Nose started to rant and struggle alarmingly. Temmi shook his head.

'Surely we're not going to release him, are we? Not after the way he plotted against us.'

'We can't very well leave him here,' said Ollimun. He knelt down beside the nets. 'I need you to give me your word, Tin Nose, that there will be a truce between us. You must promise not to harm us in any way—by wolf, by sword, or by hand, and for that you will be given your freedom.'

There was a long pause then—'Oh, very well. I promise you will come to no harm from me until . . . until there is another full moon in the sky. I give my word on it as a true lord of the High Witchlands.'

'And you promise to keep your wolf under control?'

'Yes—yes,' he snapped. 'Now am I to be released or not?'

'Do you think we can trust him?' asked Soy doubtfully.

'For all his faults, Tin Nose *is* a man of his word,' Agna was forced to admit.

'Come on, let's get those nets off him,' said Temmi. He suddenly jerked back. 'Ugh! Don't they smell disgusting?'

In his armour, Tin Nose was as helpless as a turtle on its back: the nets tangled around his shoulder spikes (which now seemed more foolish than menacing). To save time they cut him free; then it needed all hands to lift him, raising him bit by bit until, like a statue, he was finally upright.

He thrust on his helmet bad-temperedly and thought it beneath him to thank anyone.

Having rescued him, the rescuers now stood back to let Tin Nose deal with Frostbite. The brute was so furious that he threatened to bite any hand that came near him, so it was just as well for Tin Nose that he wore armour.

Bristling, Frostbite sprang free of the final net and stood growling and shaking himself. The sight of him on the loose was enough to send Cush soaring up twice as high, whimpering with fright.

'Now remember your promise,' said Ollimun, 'and see that it is kept.'

Tin Nose scowled, but his sword remained firmly in its scabbard; and calling Frostbite to him, he held the wolf tightly by his scruff.

Led by Ollimun and his wand-light, the strange company of friends and enemies quickly retraced its steps down the long sloping tunnel. Cold air met them as they stepped out.

Soy was puzzled. He squinted up at the sky. 'What, has the moon gone down already?' he said.

'No,' replied Ollimun slowly. 'The darkness has nothing to do with the moon. It is a passing shadow. See. *Grimskalk has returned.*'

Chapter Fifteen

From one edge of the sky to the other, a deep rumbling shook the air, and the smell of dragon was strong. Everyone stood looking up, and even Frostbite forgot his snappishness for a moment, the fur along his back beginning to rise.

Then slowly—slowly and grandly—Grimskalk beat her wings and the moon and stars were revealed beneath them. Her eyes in two green beams swept over the land and her fang-clustered jaws opened like the entrance to a cave. Had she wanted, she could have bitten a hill in half and afterwards spat out boulders like crumbs.

The goblins were tiny insects in her shadow.

Temmi watched them. Their torches burned

brightly, and here and there gold and silver caught the light. Some goblins struggled to carry heavy thrones (thinking they would be fine armchairs in their dismal caves, and that their caves would be turned instantly into palaces). The thrones were strapped upon their backs and were so large that it appeared as if they had sprouted bandy legs of their own then decided how nice it would be to go out on a midnight stroll.

The wind carried the sound of goblin voices. Temmi heard how they shrieked, half in terror and half in defiance, swarming over icy rocks towards the forest where they believed they would be safe.

Temmi knew that whenever she wished, Grimskalk could crush them and the trees flat.

'If only you give back the treasure, the dragon will leave you in peace,' he muttered, surprised to find himself concerned for what became of them.

'Let the dragon eat her fill, it will serve those Underworld traitors right,' said Tin Nose harshly.

Temmi threw him a look.

'Well, why should I care what happens to them?' said Tin Nose staring back haughtily.

'They are still heading for the forest,' said Soy.

'Give up the treasure,' said Temmi again. But he might as well have said, give up your lives—for goblins are such greedy grasping creatures. Already in their minds they saw the precious things as rightfully theirs and the dragon as the thief. They slipped and scrambled; dropped treasure causing endless squabbles around the rabble's edge.

And all the while Grimskalk showed great patience, circling her mountain and circling high over the goblins' heads. When she passed over Temmi he felt the rush of wind almost suck him up. He saw plumes of snow fly off the mountain peak; and the green beams that restlessly patrolled the land sent every shadow swirling.

That was when Temmi felt Cush push between his legs, head low and frightened. A dragon in the air, a wolf on the ground . . . it was all too much for a young bear like him.

The goblins had almost reached the forest. They were so close that their big feet trampled the shadows of the tallest trees. This was the moment when Grimskalk's patience came to an end. Throwing back her head she brought it plunging forward, breathing out flames of ice. The flames struck the land. Instantly they froze. And a wall of ice cut off the goblins' escape.

This first shot was in warning.

She rose up again leaving the goblins to squawk and squabble and slip and shove. Now they did not bother to pick up what loot they dropped; but clinging still to what they had, they rushed to get around the wall.

They were never going to get away. Grimskalk dived. Ice blue flames flickered—then roared—then set solid. In one breath she had caught the entire goblin army, trapping it in a tomb of thick ice, some so deeply buried that they were nothing more than ghostly shapes. Others, nearer to the surface, held up their arms in surprise, a yell frozen on their lips, and gold suspended in mid air as it tumbled to the ground.

Grimskalk, satisfied and tired out by her long night flight, returned to her mountain. She curled herself around it as if it were a comfortable pillow and shut her eyes.

The green beams of light vanished and the only sound just then was the wind's murmur . . . until Temmi heard the distinct scrape of a blade being drawn. He leapt round quickly, but was too late. Tin Nose stood with his sword in his hand; while Frostbite, springing onto a rock, crouched ready to attack.

'What is this, some kind of trick?' shouted Temmi. 'Tin Nose, you promised. You gave your word there would be a truce between us!'

An icy smile glimmered. 'My word is not

broken; I promised a truce between us until there was another full moon in the sky. Well, look up. Look into Frostbite's eyes. Can you not see another full moon in each of them, reflecting the one above?'

Soy shook his head and groaned. 'We should have known better. We should have left him behind in the nets.'

'You are too mean, Tin Nose!' cried Agna.

'My sword is meaner, as are Frostbite's claws and fangs. If you know what's best for you, you will do exactly what I say. Boy, keep that bear quiet, its growling is more bothersome than frightening. You—the wizard—lay your wand on the ground. As for the rest of you, you will throw down any weapons you have, where I can see them. *Hurry*. Why do you stand there grinning at me?'

'Because, Tin Nose,' answered Temmi, 'you've jumped in too soon. *You* should be the one who lays down his weapon. And *you* should see that *your* animal behaves. Look behind you.'

'What at? Rocks? Sky? Snow?'

'I am not a rock,' said a voice, 'although I do feel a little boulder.'

'I am not sky,' said another voice, 'although some may look up to me.'

157

'I am not snow,' said a third voice, 'although I can make your blood run cold.'

Turning clumsily in his armour, Tin Nose was startled to see heads bob up from behind every rock up to the top of the gorge, until an army of children had appeared, their bows and arrows aimed at him or his wolf. One of their number jumped up and stood with his hands on his hips, grinning at Soy. It was Mau. Only Mau could be so reckless. Soy's delight at seeing *him* was better disguised.

'Mau, what are you doing here? You should be resting. You should be taking care of yourself . . . ' He ran out of words, then added despairingly, 'Sometimes I think you don't have a single sensible bone in your whole body.'

'Don't nag, little brother. I've already had that song sung to me a hundred times by Ollah. I'm fine. Honestly. I could do a somersault. Besides, how could I stay in bed knowing you were out here amongst dragons and goblins?' He laughed. 'Tell me, aren't you a little bit glad to see me?' He leapt down and noticed Ollimun. 'Thank you, wizard, you mended me rather well. In fact we were on your tail half a day after you left and might have caught you too had we not run into that terrible storm.'

'Whatever you owed me, you have paid back by coming to our rescue,' said Ollimun graciously.

Mau glanced across at Tin Nose. '*Oh, him.* That just makes us even for what his wolf did to me. Who knows, I may yet make that monster into a fur coat and hang his tail from my hat for fun.'

'While you are wondering whether to or not,' said Ollimun, 'have some rope thrown down. I'm sure Tin Nose will be kind enough to muzzle his wolf so he doesn't go biting anyone else. Oh, and do be careful with your own fingers, Tin Nose. I should hate you to have an accident.'

Glaring savagely, Tin Nose obeyed. Frostbite shook his head furiously, trying to throw off the rope, but Mau only made Tin Nose tie it tighter.

'That's much better,' he said inspecting it.

'I must have a few words,' Ollimun told Temmi. 'Help me up on to this rock.' Temmi steadied the wizard's arm as he climbed up. Once everyone could see him, he began to speak, his voice ringing out clearly.

'Listen to me, everyone. Tonight we will camp at the castle and tomorrow we will set off for your village. But let me warn you, if you wish to return home safely you will leave any treasure you see lying in the snow. And better that it should. If you are tempted, even by the smallest trinket, it brings with it the curse of the dragon.'

'You can trust us,' said Mau. 'We do not take what isn't ours. We aren't goblins.'

Temmi helped Ollimun down again and in a long straggling line they wound their way back to Castle Surewall. In the fading moonlight, jewels sparkled like odd little flowers, and every step trod brooches and bracelets underfoot.

And Tin Nose noticed these things—he saw how they glittered; and in his mind a plan glittered just as brightly.

Pretending to stumble, he fell to his knees. He made a convincing show of it, cursing aloud. But when he got up, there was a secret smile on his face . . . and a small ruby ring clenched in his hand. And then, when no one was watching, it was the easiest thing in the world to drop it into Temmi's pocket.

Chapter Sixteen

Back at the castle the wizard and his young companions should have been worn out. But they weren't. So as Mau and a few other older boys marched Tin Nose and Frostbite away to find a secure place where they could stand guard over them, Ollimun led the others up on to the main wall; Cush following them there, climbing one step at a time, yawning and too tired to fly (but not yet willing to let Temmi out of his sight in case another wolf or dragon appeared).

The wall-top gave a clear view over the land, the light of the setting moon now grey.

'See, somebody is busy,' said Ollimun pointing.

Below, among snowdrifts taller than themselves,

moved a number of grublings. They looked odd in their dark glasses. As small as young children, they could be seen scurrying after the goblins' tracks, picking up whatever had been dropped in their panic to escape. They worked in silence, the breeze blowing their fine hair, and their footprints so small and shallow that they hardly left a shadow in the snow.

Further off, Grimskalk clung large and terrible to her mountain. She slept restlessly, every now and again lifting her head in the direction of the castle, her nostrils twitching eagerly.

'I suppose she's dreaming she's flying,' said Temmi watching her. 'Cush is the same when he dreams, aren't you, boy?'

Cush lumbered forward, sleepily wagging his tail when Temmi tweaked his ear.

Just then a voice called up to them from the courtyard below. It was Mau.

'Have you found somewhere good and strong to hold the prisoners?' Ollimun asked him.

'Yes, the base of the second tower over there. It has no windows and three of our best lads are guarding the door. Don't worry. They won't take any nonsense from them.'

'Good,' said Temmi. 'Was Tin Nose angry when you showed him his cell?'

'No,' answered Mau. 'In fact the opposite. He bowed and thanked me.'

'*Thanked you,*' said Agna astonished. She frowned. 'Why should he do that? It makes me feel uneasy when I hear that Tin Nose is behaving so well.'

'I expect he knows he is beaten, that's all,' said Temmi with a shrug—and perhaps a little more careless than he should have been.

Agna was not so sure. 'Tin Nose is far too arrogant for that idea even to cross his mind. We ought to be extra careful. I wouldn't be surprised if Tin Nose isn't plotting something even now.'

Temmi smiled at her. 'That's the cold getting into your bones and making you see things for the worst. What can possibly happen now? Let's go and see if our fire is still burning and thaw you out a little.'

The fire, which they had left many hours ago, was low, but they quickly built it up again. Agna liked the way Temmi fussed over her, getting lots of furs to keep her warm before settling down himself. Ollimun was already snoring, and Cush, curled up asleep, made a living pillow.

'I'm going to find Mau,' whispered Soy, creeping away. 'If I know him he'll have forgotten to take the wizard's medicine.'

Temmi tried to wish him a goodnight, but when he did all that came out was a yawn. A moment later he was asleep.

Temmi sat up with a sharp intake of air that made his head spin, the roar that had awoken him still ringing in his ears.

'Ollimun—what was *that*?' he cried—and needlessly so, because only a dragon's roar could make the ground tremble and the walls groan and wake every sleeping creature for miles around, even those deep in burrows beneath the snow.

Agna sat clutching her furs to her chin.

'Grimskalk sounds angry. She sounds as if she wants to pick a quarrel with someone. It can't be with us, can it? We've done her no harm.'

'No harm unless . . . ' came the wizard's grave voice. '*Someone has disobeyed me*. Someone has stolen from the dragon and foolishly ignored the curse.'

He was up immediately. He struck his wand on the floor and had light. Without waiting for the others he rushed out. Agna and Temmi tumbled from their beds after him; Cush, growling and bristling, went too.

In the main courtyard they practically ran into Soy and Mau.

'Grimskalk has turned against us!' cried Soy pointing up at the dragon circling in the sky.

'We know,' said Ollimun bluntly. 'There is a thief in the camp. Spread the word. Tell everyone if they have anything belonging to the dragon to get rid of it at once. If not, we will not leave this castle alive.'

He sounded so sure of that, that Temmi's hair prickled.

Mau grabbed Soy's arm and they began running away.

'We'll do what we can, wizard,' called Mau. Then they were gone.

The dragon came swooping in, silent and full of menace; her eyes lighting the way. Swiftly green light flooded the courtyard so that all the ruined pillars down the sides glowed shadowless and the darkest corners were suddenly revealed. From deep inside her, Grimskalk roared again—her jaw and nostrils shooting out jets of freezing vapour that instantly turned to ice, man-sized icicles forming whiskers upon her chin.

'Run for cover!' ordered Ollimun, his words almost swept away in the hurricane of wing beats that fanned the snow until it raced and snaked like forest fire smoke.

For the dragon now hovered right over the

courtyard, her beams fixed upon the little fleeing group. She measured their distance. Then with a gentle nudge of her tail she deliberately toppled a tower. It crashed down in a long line, headed straight for Temmi and his friends.

Stones bounced wildly ahead, overtaking them—smashing against the wall.

Temmi, Agna, and Cush made it through the nearest doorway; Ollimun a heartbeat slower. The towers domed roof struck the ground last. And Ollimun, a step away from being safe inside the room with the others, was struck on the head by a flying tile. He fell to the ground at Agna's feet. Then a choking cloud of dust swirled in as crashing rubble packed solid in the doorway, blocking it up to the top.

'*Ollimun!*'

Temmi raced across. To his horror he saw a dark patch of blood on Ollimun's head. Agna knelt on the other side of the wizard, her hands pressed to her cheeks. Ollimun's eyes kept opening and closing. They stayed closed longer each time.

Reaching inside his pocket, Temmi pulled out his handkerchief; with it came something else. Something that gleamed briefly before it rolled across the floor and was lost in the shadows.

167

'What was that? It looked like a ring,' whispered Agna.

'But I never put it there,' protested Temmi. 'Somebody else must have . . . *Tin Nose. It was Tin Nose!*' he cried, remembering the sly look on Tin Nose's face after he seemed to take a tumble.

Ollimun fought to speak, choking on the dust, 'D-dragon treasure. Return. D-do it at once.'

'But you're hurt, Ol—'

'*Leave me. Go.* Or the d-dragon destroys us all.'

Temmi stared wildly at Agna.

'The ring—where did it go?'

'I don't know,' she uttered. 'But we have to find it.'

In the fading light of Ollimun's wand they scrambled on all fours. The dust made it more difficult. In their haste they kept picking up rocks by mistake and angrily hurling them aside. Cush searched too, his nose just then ten times more useful than Temmi's eyes. He sniffed at a crack in the floor, scrabbled at it with his claws then gave an excited yap.

'What, have you found it, boy?' cried Agna joyfully. She and Temmi were immediately at his side. Deep in the crack, Temmi could make out a faint glimmer.

'Let me,' said Agna. 'My fingers are smaller than yours.'

Without protest, Temmi allowed himself to be pushed aside. He lifted his eyes as the dragon roared overhead. He knew Grimskalk would smash down every wall to get what was hers. It is how dragons are—the way they are born to be. Grimskalk simply wouldn't be able to help herself.

'Got it!'

Agna's triumphant yell put an end to Temmi's thoughts. He took the ring from her and they crawled back to Ollimun's side.

'We've found it, Ollimun,' he said.

'It must be r-returned. Must b-be. It is t-too late to do anything else.'

Temmi did not hesitate.

'I'll fly on Cush to the dragon's mountain,' he said stoutly.

Ollimun managed a single nod. 'As long as it r-reaches the mountain . . . Take it to the m-mountain. Don't worry . . . It is n-not s-special . . . It is n-not like Icicle—the grublings will find its home . . . But you—you m-must get it to the mountain first . . . And listen, Temmi—t-take my wand w-with you.'

'Your wand? But it serves you.'

169

'*Take it*. I give it to y-you, b-boy . . . Temmi . . . You are its master now . . . '

Ollimun closed his eyes and they did not open again, a sun and a moon where each eye had been. Temmi leapt to his feet.

'Wand, get here!' he commanded.

The wand did not come.

Temmi crossed to it and snatched it up. He could feel the wand trying to pull away. He did not let go, and the more determined he was, the less the wand fought against him.

Cush was more agreeable. He came at his name and let Temmi climb on to his back. At the far end of the once grand room, through a haze of dust, appeared a magnificent round window. Its colourful glass was long gone; and through it Temmi saw the dragon's mountain stand like a single fang.

He pointed to it. 'There, Cush. Fly me there and as quickly as you can.'

Cush understood. He lumbered towards the window, going faster and faster. Temmi gripped him with his knees; in one hand he clutched the ring, while the wand was tucked beneath his arm like a lance.

Suddenly Cush's wings opened. Agna shouted something encouraging—then Temmi was free of the castle, tilting over broken roofs; the thin raw air shockingly cold.

'Good boy, Cush. Well done.' Temmi was half laughing, half crying, his feelings so mixed up.

But if he thought his troubles behind him, he was wrong. Sensing that something had happened, Grimskalk soared up and hung in the air, her nostrils twitching, and her green beams cutting the darkness as they reached beyond the castle's walls. Temmi peered back and was almost blinded by them.

'Oh no! She's spotted us.' Without meaning to be harsh he gave a kick with his heels. 'Go, Cush! Go like the wind!'

Cush didn't need to be told. The eerie green light and the roar that followed added an extra wing beat to every ten. But he was neither a big bear nor a fully grown one. He was tired and panting and already finding Temmi's weight a burden.

The dragon came after them. Black wings, fangs, beaming eyes, and claws. Silently, like a dark cloud, she passed over them, and the invisible rush of air nearly bowled Cush from the sky. Then Temmi remembered Ollimun's wand. Of course he didn't know how to use it, not properly as a wizard would, yet Ollimun's faith in him gave him the confidence to give it his best try.

He pointed the wand's powerful sun end at the dragon as she wheeled around and returned. Without him calling them, certain thoughts filled his head. Fire—lightning—lava—the first flash of the morning sun. And a bolt of white-hot light flew from the wand and struck the dragon on her snout. It must have only stung her at best; it must have been to her what a flea bite is to an elephant. But it worked and was enough. Startled, Grimskalk sent a ripple down her wings and rose higher. Meanwhile Temmi and Cush had come to the mountain.

'You must get higher, Cush,' pleaded Temmi. 'We must reach that hole near the top. And hurry, I don't think I can hold her off a second time.'

He could feel the muscles in Cush's neck stand out as he used every last bit of strength. His wings cupped the air, and his body trembled. It was so hard, yet still Temmi willed him on. Just a little bit more . . . Just a little bit more, Cush.

The mountain burned in the angry green light of Grimskalk's unblinking glare. Slowly her mouth opened. Frost flames bubbled and boiled along her jaw. No longer would she be played with—no longer would she be insulted on her very own mountain. The time had come to give that thief his lesson.

'Higher, Cush! A few strokes more should do it . . . That's it! That's it, boy. Now keep it steady.'

Temmi knew he had just one shot with the ring. The hole was large but, if anything, it was the distance between them that would be his downfall. He reached back his arm, Cush struggling not to lose height. Then with all his might Temmi hurled the ring. He saw it gleam as it flew. He saw it begin to drop. He watched in dismay as it struck the lip of the hole . . . And . . . And . . . after a heart stopping moment in which it might have tumbled either way, it fell into the mountain.

'We've done it, Cush! The ring is returned!'

Cush gladly wheeled aside, gathering speed sharply as he glided away. The green beams did not follow. Glancing back, Temmi saw the dragon settle herself back upon her mountain. She was content.

As Cush came in to land in the courtyard, Temmi bounded off his back. He staggered slightly as he found his feet, then ran over to where Soy, Mau, and a large group of children were working to clear the rubble that trapped Agna and Ollimun.

Temmi ran up to the top of the heap and shouted, 'Agna—are you all right?'

'Temmi!' squealed a muffled voice. 'Did you manage to get the ring back safely?'

'Yes, yes. But what about you?'

'I'm fine.'

'And Ollimun?'

'I've bandaged his head as best I can. Temmi . . . he is going to be all right?'

'He's got to be,' said Temmi fiercely. 'Now let's get you dug out of there.'

He lent a hand, working harder than anyone else. Soy and Mau, working alongside, told him that nobody else had been hurt in the dragon attack—but Tin Nose and Frostbite were gone. It hadn't been difficult. It seemed they took advantage of the confusion they had caused, and slipped silently away.

'We found boot and wolf prints heading north,' said Mau, pulling a face as he tugged at a large chunk of stone. 'I've a good mind to track them down and turn that wolf into a coat after all. A metal nose might make a good trophy on my wall too.'

'Oh, let them go,' said Temmi helping him with the troublesome stone. 'They can do us no harm. But make sure you have a guard in place just to be on the safe side. Now *heave*—'

The stone moved and tumbled down the heap of rubble. A gap was revealed. And there, peering out through it, was the pale, worried face of Agna.

Chapter Seventeen

Dawn arrived. The sky was streaked like old ice when many hands helped to carry Ollimun from the castle. He groaned as they set him down on one of Mau's sledges and strapped him on for his own safety, with furs to keep out the cold.

'I don't know if it is good for him to travel so soon,' said Temmi chewing his lip. 'He is so weak, the sledge ride may cost him what little strength he has left.'

'He can't very well stay here at the castle,' said Agna bluntly.

Mau was more understanding. 'Don't you worry about the journey,' he said patting Temmi's shoulder. 'I will drive as smoothly as I can. I know the best short-cuts; and if you need quiet I will stop the foxes barking.'

Temmi smiled at him blandly, Mau was so anxious to help.

Because Ollimun took up so much room, and because they were one sledge short, Soy and a group of others set off on foot for the cave where the abandoned fox team was tethered.

'We'll soon catch you up,' shouted Soy. 'My foxes will be eager for a little exercise.'

'You see you take care,' replied Mau playing the part of the big brother. 'Just you remember that Tin Nose and that wolf of his are about in the forest somewhere.'

In answer, Soy drew an arrow from his quiver and slotted it into his bow. He did it so quickly that it might have been done by magic. 'I'll be ready for him or, come to that, any stray goblins missed by the dragon.'

'We best go now,' said Temmi striding up and sounding brisk.

Mau nodded. 'Of course. Take care, little brother,' he called a final time, crossing to his sledge.

Soy waved back with his mitten and stood watching as Mau cried 'Kai-or!' And the sledges set off.

Temmi and Agna rode with Ollimun. Cush flew alongside. Later, when he was bored with flying, he did little tricks to attract Temmi's attention, hoping to win a smile or a friendly word. But Temmi's mind was on other matters.

'Watch out,' he growled at every bump along the way.

For four days and many long dull hours they travelled. Across frozen lakes, through silent forests, past banks of snow. And if Ollimun *did* open his eyes it was for a moment to murmur 'Water'; and taking a sip he fell straight back into a deep sleep once more. Temmi worried all the time, the wizard was so pale: the tattooed moon and sun had blurred and sunken with his eyes, so those who did not know would mistake them for bruises.

Then late on the fourth day the Eckmo's village came into sight, a ring of snowmen standing silently on guard around it. Small figures with lanterns ran out from the passageways until a large group had formed to give the returning sledges a noisy welcome. 'Home,' said Mau, pushing down his hood and calling back to them. Temmi glanced at Ollimun. He had begun to sweat, and he struggled in his sleep to throw off his furs. Temmi doubted whether he could have travelled much further.

Drawing to a halt, Mau ordered the sledges be unhitched and Ollimun be carried to the domed meeting place; sending others running ahead to make up a bed and throw extra logs on the fire.

Ollimun, muttering and thrashing wildly, was difficult to manage. Twice they nearly dropped him before at last setting him down.

They did all they could to make him comfortable. Agna mopped his face with a rag— and as she did, Temmi noticed she kept glancing up at him. Clearly there was something on her mind.

'I don't know, Temmi . . . ' she said, quietly going on with her work. 'There isn't much more I can do, and he's getting so weak I don't think he can fight on for himself. So . . . maybe it's up to you to help him now. You—*and magic*.'

Temmi's mouth fell open in astonishment. 'What's that you say? Magic? But how? *You* know more about magic than I do, you used to live in the castle of a witch.'

'Yes, but *I'm* not a witch, am I? And you have a wand, Ollimun gave it to you because he saw you have the talent to use it. So use it!' She smiled at him encouragingly. 'Listen, Temmi, you managed well enough against the dragon. And I'm sure the wand will help you as much as it can.'

'You think it will?' asked Temmi unconvinced.

'I know it will. It will not let you harm its old master.'

Temmi wished he felt as confident as Agna did. Indeed it took a great deal more persuading before he felt able to kneel down beside Ollimun and remove the wizard's belt, with all its herbs and charms attached. He tried to buckle it around himself, but needed to make an extra hole, for he hadn't the wizard's belly to hold it up. The belt felt awkward, slipping down his hips.

Agna and Mau meanwhile went to work, quickly setting out around him all the things he might need to help his magic along. Bowls, spoons, knives, a pestle and mortar, water, salt, feathers, bones . . .

Temmi gazed at them as if at a foreign language. 'I still don't know what to—'

But already the wand was moving his arm, pointing to where his enchantment should begin.

And as it began, so it progressed, Temmi soon discovering that it was far easier if he emptied his head of every thought and let the wand work through him.

This way the wand quickly got into its stride. It pointed to the right herbs and roots; tapped out measurements in pinches, spoonfuls, or mugs; and mimed stirring or chopping whenever either was required. It hovered impatiently when Temmi was slow, and did not hesitate to rap his knuckles if he did anything wrong.

'Ow!' cried Temmi throwing the wand a withering scowl.

And between them, by one helping the other, and with Temmi's confidence growing all the time, they made a strong healing potion, so all that was left to do was for Ollimun to take it.

Nervously Temmi cupped the wizard's head and dribbled a little of the potion on to his bottom lip. He waited to see what would happen. Oh . . . *nothing*. Perhaps I've poisoned him! thought Temmi in dismay. But no. After a moment the tip of the wizard's tongue appeared and licked the potion off. Then there was a long pause—and then the wizard opened his mouth a little, seeming to ask for more. Gladly Temmi tilted the bowl until the potion was completely gone.

'Agna—I think it's working,' he called, his heart leaping with joy. 'I'm sure Ollimun is trying to open his eyes.'

Before Agna could reply, she heard a bustle in one of the passageways and turned to see Soy come in with a group of tall, serious-looking adults: women and men dressed exactly the same in hooded coats and deerskin trousers; the men armed with long knives, the women with spears.

'Dad—Ma!' cried Mau leaping up.

He rushed over to carry his mother's spear.

'Be careful of your arm, Mau,' she said. 'The one that was bitten by the wolf.' Her eyes shone knowingly.

Mau glared at Soy who grinned and quickly changed the subject. 'We met up about a mile away. They've ridden back after defeating the goblins.'

'Now, Soy, I didn't say we *defeated* the goblins,' said their father good-naturedly, as he brushed frost off his raven black hair. 'I said they suddenly vanished—I hope back down into the Underworld, never to show their ugly green faces again.'

'So they will have,' said a voice. 'At least the ones that were not frozen in ice by Grimskalk. The dragon's curse is lifted, you see. We'll not be bothered by goblins for a long time to come.'

Temmi and Agna spun around and were astonished to see the speaker was Ollimun, propping himself up on his elbow. His voice sounded odd, as it can do if someone is allowed to sleep for too long.

Soy's father crossed over to him. 'We have been told something of that curse, as we have been told something of *you*, wizard. When you are well enough we must hear the story properly.' He noticed Agna and Temmi standing nearby. 'Ah, you must be the other strangers Soy told us about—and the bear with wings . . . So it wasn't from your imagination after all, Soy . . . We thank you all—especially you, wizard. We wish you speedy health. I would offer you the services of our wise woman, but your boy here seems to be taking excellent care of you.'

'Oh he is,' agreed Ollimun heartily.

Soy's father gestured towards the wand in Temmi's hand. 'Who knows, when you have finished your training, lad, you might become as good a wizard as your master.'

'But I'm not training to be a wi—' began Temmi.

But Ollimun interrupted. 'He'll make a fine wizard, have no doubt on that.'

Soy's father smiled, nodded, and moved away to speak to his sons. Ollimun winked and grinned stupidly at Temmi, showing every one of his long, yellow, mule-like teeth.

'What are you up to, wizard?' asked Agna suspiciously.

'Me? Why, nothing. But what about it, Temmi? How would you like it if I had words with your father when we return to your village? How would you like the chance to learn the ways of a wizard?'

Temmi didn't even think about it. 'I would like it very much indeed,' he said.

'Good, good. Then that is agreed . . . Now don't just stand there—fetch me some fresh water *and* a proper pillow. Oh, and give me back my wand before you start getting ideas about keeping it.'

Temmi raised his eyebrows. 'Back to his old self again,' he said to Agna, and they laughed and couldn't be more pleased.

Later, when the meeting place was crowded with adults and children, Soy's father led the humming. It sounded very different with grown-up voices added to it, richer and more complicated, with many more strands of sound.

Listening, Temmi leant back against Cush, feeling his warmth through his fur. The humming gradually changed. Without him realizing, it stopped rolling along like a river and became more like the drone of swarming bees. Temmi tried to imagine himself as a wizard, robed and with a wand of his own. *Temmi the wizard* . . . The thought pleased him so much it gave him a warm glow inside. Now the humming worked its way into his head; he almost felt he was flying through sound. He closed his eyes and smiled. Perhaps he would join in with his own voice. And this he did. Although no one heard it in the dream of his deep, contented steep.

Temmi and the Flying Bears
ISBN 0 19 275259 6

The Witch-Queen's guards march into Temmi's village and steal away one of the flying bear cubs—but this isn't just any cub, it's Cush, Temmi's favourite. The guards say they're taking Cush to the Witch-Queen's ice palace as a pet for the Princess.

Temmi knows he must rescue the little bear, but how can he overcome the dangers in store for him at the ice palace? What he needs are a few friends to help him in his quest . . .